Water Into Wine

Water Into Wine

Stories of Imagination and Faith

David Johnson Rowe

ISBN 978-1-387-34865-7

Proceeds from this book are given to the work of FOCI (Friends of Christ in India). For more information, visit the website at www.foci.org.

Dedication

To readers who love it when
the words become flesh
and dwell among us.

Contents

Acknowledgments

I love fiction so much that I never imagined writing it myself. Plot and characters that come to such life that you never want to let go are so precious that I did not want to ruin it for even one reader.

My journey from intimidation to motivation, from writing to publishing, is only possible because of key people who kept encouraging me while wading through these stories. Sarah Milicia, Rachel Baumann and Roni Widmer were gentle first readers, keen correctors, and astute editors.

A very special thanks to Megan Brown for the cover art, *Water into Wine*. Megan perfectly captures the mystery and simplicity of Jesus' first miracle with her own imagination and faith.

We all have authors who keep us reading. I thank those who kept me writing. The short stories of Flannery O'Connor helped me to believe that great faith did not rule out great writing. Nathan Englander allows faith to permeate his writing, even while wrestling with that faith. Junot Díaz's preface to *The Best Short Stories of 2016* is the best primer for short story writing. I put pen to paper with apologies to all three.

To bookstores, coffeehouses, and readers everywhere – thank you.

A final thank you to Alida, my muse and my editor. Not many can be both, and she is so much more.

Foreword

Literature is at its most potent when it digs out the powerful fictions which govern men's lives. A powerful fiction is a discourse which time has converted into unquestionable truth, whose fantastic origin has been forgotten.

- Franz Kafka Museum, Prague

Let's remember.

- David Johnson Rowe

God's Intro: I Am

These stories are based on the assumption that I exist.

I saw graffiti on a bathroom wall at Harvard Divinity School (yes, Harvard has a Divinity School, no joke), the old line "Cogito Ergo Sum." I think, therefore I Am.

Actually, I liked the ones below it. "Cogito Ergo Spud." I think, therefore I Yam. Even better, "Cogito Ergo Sumo." I think, therefore I wrestle. I love to wrestle. Ask Jacob.

Anyway, I agree: I think, therefore I Am. And I think I Am. With Moses a few years back I thought I was pretty clear. He was up in the air about me, some doubts, some questions, some hesitation, I don't mind that. I was sending him to confront Yul Brynner, ol' Pharaoh, and naturally Moses asks me "well, who are you, exactly?"

I couldn't have given him a clearer answer. "I Am That I Am." Or, if you prefer, "I Am Who I Am." Some branding expert shortened it to "The Great I Am." All it means is, I Am, it's me. I'm the one talking to you whom you don't expect to be talking to you. So yes, my operating premise is, I exist.

Sure, some say this is all an illusion, there's no god at all. My good friend Buddha gets blamed for this but that's not where he was headed. For the most part, Siddhartha, I still call him Siddhartha, was quoting me, about attachment and such. Don't get attached to stuff, it just makes you crazy, agitated, greedy, that sort of thing. Read the

1

Ten Commandments, that's what I Am saying. Pun intended. Other than your parents, don't be so attached, don't want so badly, and don't let loose your passions on every passing thing. Focus on the right stuff, not the little stuff.

Yes, I Am. I realize that it is increasingly popular to deny that I exist, which, let's admit it, is insulting. Supposedly it is based on reason. A reasonable person, a thinking person, reasons me out of existence. I don't get that. I reason, and I still think *you* exist.

Let's face it, you're only around a short time and then, poof, you're gone. Does that mean you didn't exist? Or don't exist? Why does your reason require me not to exist? Why can't I Am and You Am and Reason Am co-exist as We Am? Really, I'm not being sarcastic. Some of you look around and say I'm not there, ergo, I Am not. Tell me this: How many times have I looked around and not found you present and accounted for? There's the difference. I'm missing, you dismiss me. You're missing, I find you.

What I do understand is that some may find me annoying, which strikes me as a little bit of the pot hurling insults at the kettle. For the record, I Am annoying which sounds to me like proof that I exist. I Am, therefore I annoy. I annoy, therefore I Am. That's good enough for me.

And because I Am, and because I think, and because I even like to annoy, I choose to comment on some stories that you like to tell about me. Hey, I Am in the story. That's some sort of evidence, right there. I'll take that. Put me in a story.

Give me the wonderful life of Jimmy Stewart, the enduring magic of Harry Potter, the tortured heroes of Dickens; let me be Jean Valjean. Sometimes a story is not just a story.

Jesus' Iftar

L'chaim

A sign over the front door
Jesus' Iftar
it said
but it didn't seem right
with neon blinking lights
in green and red.
    A guy walks into a bar,
    old Vaudeville opening line,
    a little bread and little wine
    might take you far
    or so he said.
In a corner
we sat down together
to break the fast
eat what was broken
drink what was passed.
    We forgot to remember
    the shape of the bread
    the color of the wine
    till he looked at us
    and smiled
    "L'chaim."

*H*e walks in, a little unkempt, like a man looking for his last supper. There's that woman with him, unexpected at this late hour. A distraction. Even with the bustling about there's a sort of forced holy hush in the air, people preoccupied. Some whispering in the corner, almost conspiratorial. Everything looks set, proper, ready. Only the man seems out of place. He goes around the room, touching each person, a little too intimately. People are uncomfortable. They move away from him. He doesn't get the hint.

Some treat him like the Alzheimered favorite uncle who wandered in from the street, deference mixed with annoyance. He's an odd fellow on the best of days, they often joke about it, and are looking forward to a night free of duty, fueled with just enough wine to loosen the shackles of history closing in. They knew it, and denied it, all at the same time.

"Why is this night different from all other nights?" the youngest one asks.

"Because we don't have to work tomorrow," the burly fellow laughs, pleased at his own good humor. "Here, pour," he says, wanting to get the night started. He likes the sound of his own voice. Somewhere he had learned to swagger audibly. The holy hush gives way to smug.

The man clears his throat, the way a teacher does to get attention for the day's lesson. But no one is in a mood for lessons. Even with the night's rites and rituals getting warmed up, they aren't focused. One of the group looks like he is trying to ease out the door. That one gestures toward the man's companion with his chin, an act full of contempt. "You know she can't sit there. This isn't for everyone."

He doesn't look up, but speaks, "That's right, 100%. This evening is only for the righteous. 'Members Only,' I like that." Then looking around at all of us he adds, "Write that down. Members only. Our own brand, don't you think? The perfect. The Chosen. A few good men. That's why I set only twelve places."

"Thirteen," someone corrects.

"Twelve." Ah, someone is excluded. They like that.

"Ok. Twelve. Surely I ..." one of us stammers, only to be interrupted.

"Don't you mean, 'surely not I'?" Had he caught the whiff of betrayal in the air? Did he know who was about to deny him? Or deny denying him? Or those who were out the door in more ways than one?

They catch the edge in his voice. "Uh, these twelve, the, well, the chosen. Who, exactly?"

"Many."

Silence.

"Which ones?" a little too nervously.

"Nelson Mandela. Mother Teresa. St. Francis. Rosa Parks."

He looks at them; they look at each other quizzically. As dense as they could be, they knew their apocalyptics. He put them to sleep many a night with his futuristic, tall tales. His future was always bigger than their imagination.

"Lauren Bacall. Billie Joe Armstrong."

"You're pulling my leg!"

"Am I? They make me happy."

Ok. This is absurd, but we can be absurd back. Someone shouts, "Lauren Bacall. Billie Joe Armstrong. Fine. Why not the whole band? And Bogart."

"Good. The whole band. And Bogart."

Silence. Embarrassed, perturbed, hard to read. But silence. Till....

"Darwin, Shakespeare. And Kafka."

"The Metamorphosis guy? The cockroach?"

"Yes, Metamorphosis, he gets it. And it was a beetle, not that it matters. And Christopher Hitchens."

"Christopher Hitchens. Christopher Hitchens! Are you doing this to annoy us, or to annoy him?"

"Mostly to annoy me. I like to be nudged from time to time. Oh, the Good Thief, and his friend, the Other Thief."

"You're cra– !"

He smiles, and shakes his finger. "Don't say that. In my book, saying is the same as doing, but saying it makes it seem worse, so don't say it. You'll live to regret it."

Reprimand noted. Alright, we'll play along. One of us notes, "I think we're over twelve. You said you set only twelve places. You're over, and you haven't mentioned us."

"Huh." It is a noncommittal "huh," followed by a non-committal "sorry." "Well, the people of Tibet. And Mexicans."

"Mexicans? Why so political?"

This earns an exasperated laugh. "Everything I do is political. Bethlehem was political. Passover is political.

Crucifixion is political. Talking with you tonight is political. Where do you want me to stop? With you, before you? After you?"

He's out of his mind. Along with all the individual denial denying and betrayal denying going on out loud, there's a lot going on in stage whispers and in our heads. Surely someone wants to say, out loud, *Forgive me, Lord, you are out of your freakin' mind.* Ok, we get it, this is some sort of special night. Portentous is a good word. Foreshadowing. We get it. But nobody tells him he's out of his freakin' mind, not straight on.

He's been troubled of late, like some internal pressure is building. Opposition is clearer, there are spies around, our own group is splintering. We are no longer the Kum Ba Yah group of the Sermon on the Mount days. It feels like the end times, without the victory. As Judas said the other day, this is not what I signed on for.

The young man closest to him stands up and, as if to speak for the group, declares,

"Lord, you know we love you. When others put their head to the plough and looked back, when others grew weary of the road, when others refused to turn the other cheek, when others came up with excuse after excuse, we never wavered."

"Publicly," he reminds us.

The young man nods. "Publicly. Sure, we each had our moments, doubts, questions. Mostly, you helped us work them through. So, we're here. I won't say it's all clear as day, but it is pretty much clear as day. Once you set yourself toward Jerusalem the good old days were over. We could see it in your eyes. Worse, we could see it in the eyes of the Roman soldiers. Our Victory Parade last Sunday sealed the deal, don't you think?"

People are nodding, vigorously.

"And that scene in the Temple was ugly. Whether it was the right thing to do or not, and it felt right, we crossed a line."

Murmurs of approval? Disapproval? Resignation. Murmurs.

"And therefore?" Jesus looks around the room.

"And therefore, be nice to us. Your sarcasm. Silly answers. Broad hints of criticism. We don't deserve that. We know you have some future in mind, you talk about 'the kingdom' all the time. And we know it's not exactly palaces and chariots and gold chalices, but it is something, and it is near, you said that. Let's be honest, we've given our lives to it, to you."

"Not yet." The man smiles at us, not a gotcha smile, not patronizing. Actually, a very tender smile. Respectful. I look around, not sure that it registered with everyone. "Not yet," he had said. Someday down the road, soon, I think, we will remember and wonder how we missed it. For me, I hear it as tender. "Not yet." Portentous. Foreshadowing.

The burly fellow, slowly seething, challenges him. "Come on, be serious. We're here. We're still with you. And you lumped us in with film noir, punk rock, and whole countries of untouchables. You're making light of this. Of us."

He jumps on that, declaring, "A: I like them. B: I like you. They go together, A and B. And C: trust me on this, I do not make light of this."

Deathly silence. Everyone in their own world.

After an eternity, he picks up a big piece of bread and begins tearing it, slowly, and rather poignantly gives some to each of us.

"I'm sorry if this hasn't been clear. Where we are headed. How it will turn out. Who wins. Maybe we've danced around the obvious a bit too much."

He carefully gathers up all the left over pieces and touches them. "This is me." I look at the bread, broken. Maybe if he had been clearer none of us would be here tonight.

He sighs. This man who had entered this room so humbly, then pushed us so abruptly, this combination of awkward holiness and inner strength, now seems so fragile.

Catching us staring, he even more dramatically picks up a wine skin and slowly pours the wine into his cup from some height. "Don't forget this," he says. "Don't forget me."

We had eaten the bread briskly, as on command. But we drink slowly, very, very intentionally. We pour for ourselves and for one another. Frankly, we pour more than we drink, as if the pouring is the purpose. We pour from different heights. We stare into the cup, even while sipping. We eat the crumbs around us. Something is going on.

He stands, takes the woman by the hand, goes to the door, looks back and seems to decide, "Let's go."

Epilogue

Jesus once told us how it all began with a fast. He had gone into the wilderness for forty days, alone, without anything. He sat, he walked, he talked out loud. To himself, we asked? No, he told us. He didn't talk to himself.

Time went by, the clouds took shape, storms came and went, he climbed rocks, slept in caves. He sat, he walked, he listened. Listened to what, we asked? To whom, he told us.

The fast went on. The Tempter came. Evil in all its glory, with all its power, stood beside him, walked with him, sat with him, talked with him. He talked to you, we asked? You listened to him? Yes, he talked to me, he told us. No, he had not listened to him.

That fast went on for forty days, but it didn't end. His withdrawal from delights, the consistent presence of evil, the walking and talking with unseen powers, the push and pull of golden opportunities, the gathering clouds continued for three years. Until that night, with broken bread and poured wine, the fast ended.

Tracy Lee

Day One

*I*t was summer, late 1960s. I met Tracy Lee after a mad scramble from the subway, the "El," we called it. When a subway comes up for air it ceases to be sub anything. It is now elevated. Hence, the El. In my neighborhood, the tracks of the El covered Jamaica Avenue like an urban rainforest canopy. It seemed beautiful, even natural.

The subway system is the great equalizer. You may get on at different stops and get off at different stops, but in between you are closer than family. Tracy Lee and I lived on the same line but in different worlds. There was nobody like him in our neighborhood, and none of me in his. That's the way it was. As if some magnetic field drew likes to one side or the other, like to like. It hadn't yet occurred to folks that unlikes from one side could cross over to unlikes on the other and like it. But we all met on the El.

Riding the El took you into the lives of thousands of New Yorkers whose apartments faced out eye-level to the straphangers. You rode the El hanging onto a strap, looking out the windows directly into the living rooms, kitchens, bedrooms of the great Queens blue-collar middle class. All of Archie Bunker's poorer relatives lived along the El, their intimacies watched by riders passing through their world for ten seconds, twice a day.

I thought of them as neighbors. The men in t-shirts, the old fashioned kind; always too small for bellies too big, always white, always looking worked-in, lived-in, sweated-in. The women in housedresses and rollers. All with cigarettes.

The summer was hot, asphalt jungle hot; nobody had AC. People had windows, and if you were lucky, fire escapes. The fire escape was like a patio for families who lived their lives as a reality show for the endless flow of passing strangers on the El.

The 60s. Maybe it should be in all caps: THE SIXTIES. It really was a singular unit of time. I mean, a decade is just an artifice, right? 1974 to 1984 is a decade. But nobody thinks of it that way. The 60s, however, all just flowed together, the good, the bad, the ugly. Music, revolution, sex, peace, drugs, Vietnam, the Rolling Stones, memories.

I remember the 1964 World's Fair right next to the brand new Shea Stadium, home of the still-new New York Mets. You could take the El to the World's Fair, too. It was an incredible jumble of ideas and images and experiences. GE robots, the fire dancers of Polynesia – and the Pieta. From Rome they had brought the honest-to-God Pieta, Michelangelo's stunning marble sculpture, for the Vatican pavilion. Awestruck visitors like me viewed the Pieta from moving sidewalks which glided past this emotional marvel, allowing us to gaze for maybe twenty seconds. You didn't have to be Catholic or an art lover to feel the pathos of Mary cradling the dead Christ just taken down from the cross. This was life, real and true, in all its pain, in all its glory, in all its beauty, in all its heartache. Just like riding the El past folks on their fire escapes or inside their little apartments, living their lives full of pathos, and love, cigarettes, beer, and TV.

By the summer of 1966, I was freshly kicked out of college, living at home, no more frat house, looking for some college to take me in and keep me out of Vietnam. Draft deferments for college only worked if you actually went to college. That subtlety had been lost on me. Evidently going to college included going to class and I never actually went to class.

So I went home, and went to work. Irony of ironies, I got a job in the salvation business. In the city, the West Side Story gangs of the 50s had long since morphed into armed camps fueled by grudges rooted in race, poverty, injustice, clan. With the city going to hell, some Brooklyn churches believed in the Bible enough to think that if everyone just had a copy it might make a difference. My job was to organize church ladies, and a few men, to visit every apartment, every house, every store – and give their occupants a free Bible, available in 150 languages.

The mayor's plan to counter the violence of that hot summer was to contain it. "Burn, baby, burn," some called the policy. When bad stuff happened, establish a perimeter, let the fires rage inside the lines and don't let it spread. But my volunteers wanted to spread what they had. They had different words for it. Good News. Gospel. Salvation. Love. Peace. Jesus. They hoped it would catch fire.

I was way out of my league, a sales manager for a product I knew nothing about. I was Saul turned into Paul minus the requisite Damascus Road conversion. I was King David writing his Psalm 51 of contrition without actually being contrite.

It was this unlikely job that had me scrambling that day from the El to the church where I met Tracy Lee. Along with *fuhgedaboutit,* Brooklyn was known for its steeples: the Borough of Churches, it was called. This church was one of the old, massive edifices that dominated the landscape. Big sanctuary, big meeting rooms, big kitchens, big everything. And in that hot summer these churches were the heartbeat of the city, the seawall against the rebellion percolating on rooftops, those tarpaper beaches where anarchy was planned.

Guys like Tracy Lee and me, do-gooders of various stripes, were the foot soldiers of the revolution, whether Jesus' or Che's. How much was real, how much was imagined, it's hard to say. In that zone of containment, we were in the container, me and Tracy Lee, and a million others, sweating bullets. And dodging them.

Tracy Lee was Vietnam Vet and Harlem Jazz fused into a human Rorschach test. Read into him what you want, beware your biases. Part Bobby Seale, part Mahatma Gandhi, part Thelonious Monk, part John Kerry. None of which he put on you. It was there for the taking.

That first day I got off the El, walked down the stairs and through the exit, looked around, and promptly set a world record for the fastest sprint by a man escaping imagined enemies. I was terrified. Arriving at the church, panting, I walked in and found my space. I set up shop, looked across the room and saw a model for urban grace under fire. He was whittling.

I pretended to be busy, very busy, with nothing to do and no one to do it with, but terribly busy. Slowly, my people began to drop in, taken aback by my disheveled youth but welcoming. New convert, they figured.

By noon I was bored. My people had come, picked up their shopping bags of scriptures, headed out to save the world. Tracy Lee's people came in a steady stream. It was like he was holding court. People sat down, leaned in, seemed to pour their hearts out, there were tears, anger, nods. They left noticeably elevated. Reminded me of times when my subway emerged from the bowels of Manhattan, transformed into the El by daylight. There was always a moment of relief. His clientele had that.

Emboldened by boredom, I went to his corner. He was whittling, again.

"Whittling?" I said, stating the obvious. "Reminds me of Boy Scouts."

"Boy Scouts taught you whittling in the city? You don't see much whittling in the city."

He went back to it, small pieces of wood, small knife, small strokes, almost tender.

"Our Scoutmaster said every city boy should be a woodsman," I said, speaking too fast. Trying to impress him with my urban jungle experience. "We did our Map Reading merit badge on the subways, tracking in Central Park, had to find sassafras to make tea, and woodcarving. 'Enjoy the woods, respect the woods,' he told us."

"Hmmm. Hmmm. Good. Did you make anything?"

"Mostly things like arrows, spears, anything you could whittle down to a tip. It did seem peaceful, whittling. What are you making?"

"A cross."

That hung in the air awhile. He whittled, I wondered. A big man whittling a small cross in a crazy city.

"You're perplexed," he said.

"It doesn't make sense," I said, which in itself doesn't make sense, but I said it, maybe more honest than I meant to be.

"Would a big cross make more sense?"

Suddenly I was aware of the crosses all around us, on walls, on tables, up above the altar, on top of the steeple, all the crosses trying to make sense of that big cross long ago. Tracy Lee bent over, reached into his bag, pulled out several crosses, placed them on the table. Some smooth, some rough, some gnarled.

"What do you do with them?"

"I give them out. Leave them places. Make people think. I left one on the El this morning."

That's when we discovered we lived on the same subway line. Different worlds, same line. We danced around the differences, comparing notes on survival of the fittest in our little containment zone. He laughed when he found out I was kicked out of college, lost my draft deferment, and now was stuck in a war zone. "Lucky I found you," he said, and sounded like he meant it. He handed me a cross, the gnarled one.

The rest of the day slipped by. My people reported in, full of joy. His people reported in, left with joy. When it was time to go he said he was staying late.

Day Two

The next morning Tracy Lee was waiting on the platform at my station. We greeted each other as men do, wordless with a thousand words expressed by eyebrows, chins, shoulders, grunts. The platform accepted him.

We found empty straps side by side, hung on them, and marveled at the drama unfolding before us through the windows. The t-shirt and the housedress seemed ready for our arrival, offering rage, exasperation, burnt toast, laughter, romance. Pretty sure we saw new life being created on a fire escape. Tracy Lee laughed.

As we got off at our stop I looked over my shoulder; there was a cross on a seat. A woman sat down, picked it up, began to weep. The door closed.

Down on the street, Tracy Lee took charge. Dressed in Army boots, camouflage jacket, knapsack over his shoulder, he looked ready for war. He was. After explaining hand signals, he showed me how to run the gauntlet of life. From the El to the mailbox, mailbox to delivery truck, behind the truck till it stops, duck into a deli, buy a coffee and a bagel, catch our breath, repeat until we reached the church.

Once inside the church, we were cool. A brotherhood. Battle tested, war weary, vets. One real. One fake. Still, I sauntered.

It was a good morning for both of us. My people checked in and out, his people checked in and out, each leaving with some version of sauntering, some of it borrowed, like mine.

During lunch he whittled me a little spear, "for old time's sake," he joked. I was in full blown hero-worship mode, accomplished without his bragging for it. Tracy Lee told stories, softly, one after another, leaving just enough pause for me to leave if I got bored. I never was. He was never the hero of his stories, never the subject or the object. It is crazy to say, but it always seemed like I was in the story. He was telling me my story, which couldn't be, he barely knew me, and, after my initial silliness, I was too awkward to say much. And I wasn't a story worth telling.

Tracy Lee was the real deal in my world as I imagined it. Street tough, Christ soft, Dad firm, gang true, bad boy made good, a Brooklyn phoenix, a Good News story with just enough of a hard edge to keep the playgrounds safe.

Reveries are meant to be broken, and the Utopia of my mind was suddenly breached by screeches of bedlam from outside. Across the street was a playground, a chain link emporium. Chain link fence, chain link nets on basketball hoops, so that even the swish of a perfect shot sounded hostile.

A girl came running into the church, shrieking. I couldn't understand her, but I heard the mayhem, shouts, curses, screams, threats, thumps. I rushed outside, ran straight to the center of the playground, shoved my way into the crowd, and pushed aside dozens of teenagers, all fully weaponized by testosterone. I was just in time to see an infuriated boy raise up a gigantic plank of wood studded with nails, and bring it crashing down on the head of an about-to-be-dead boy before him. The *thwack* of the blow rattled the chain links around us, the only sound left in the playground. We all stared, frozen by what we saw. The board had landed squarely, pounding the boy into the pavement as if he'd shrunk. But, impossibly, the nails had missed – instead, landing on either side of his cranium, embracing his head in a nail vise. Girls dropped to their knees. Non-Catholics crossed themselves. The perp backed up, all the way out the park, never taking his eye off the nails.

Everybody seemed to be waiting for something. Death. Cops. God. Instead, silence.

Still not sure what I'd seen, I bent down to the boy kneeling on the pavement with his crown of nails. Gently, I pulled it up, leaving little trails of blood leaking down where sideburns grow. He reached up to help with the final push to get it off, and I noticed he had a small cross in one hand. A few feet away Tracy Lee was hugging the girl who had come screeching into the church. There was a welt over her eye, and she stifled a sob as he put something in her hand.

With a nod of his head he indicated that we should head back to the church. I had entered the playground what, maybe ten minutes before, driven by adrenaline fueled by a faith I didn't know I had and a hero I hardly knew. I left the playground feeling spent – and adult.

Tracy Lee looked down the street at the almost-murderer, still walking backwards. "It wasn't his day to kill," he said. Then looking over his shoulder into the park at the almost-murdered, "It wasn't his day to die. Sometimes it's not your day, sometimes it is, sometimes it's contradictorily mixed. That one, maybe it was his day to die; but that other one, it wasn't his day to kill. Maybe tomorrow. But they have today."

As he opened the door to the church he fixed his eyes on me. "What are you going to do for them today?"

Frankly, I was going to sit in my little corner of the room believing in grace for the first time in my life. But none of my people were around and none of his people. Instead, Tracy Lee steered us into the sanctuary. Dark wood, stained glass heroes, gently curving pews. Protestants don't talk this way but it seemed like we had entered the Holy of Holies.

We sat down, the pew creaked, the sound reverberated. It was about to reverberate more.

"Some day, huh?" he said pointedly, turning toward me. "So you tell me, what are you going to do for them today?"

To my amazement, he took his knife out of one pocket, a piece of wood out of another, and just started whittling in the pew, wood shavings falling like indoor snowflakes in July. Like he owned the place.

Equal parts embarrassed and perplexed, I watched him whittle, and pondered his repeated question. *What are you going to do?* I thought maybe he'd say, what are *we* going to do, now that we were almost a team. Or better, he could say, here's what *I* will do with them.

Whittling is disconcerting. It is, by nature, destructive and creative. Something is being cut down to size, carved up, transformed. It must have been a hundred degrees in that sanctuary and still, I shuddered. Maybe I am being whittled. It wasn't that one boy's day to die, it wasn't that other boy's day to kill, maybe it was this boy's day to live. I shuddered again.

"Tracy Lee," I said, using his name for the first time, like we were intimates, "why didn't you, or we, you and me, why didn't we go after that boy? He was still there, just a block away, backing up step by step, like he couldn't believe...."

"We'll see," he interrupted. "I pay attention to what I can do something about. Your Jesus up there," pointing with his knife to a stained glass window, "he told folks he came for the sick, the ones that knew they were sick. Triage of the soul. I learned that over there, triage, you spend yourself where you can do some good. That boy backing away? He's flying high, feeling good, as well as well gets. He doesn't need us." I smile. "Us," he had said.

"We could have given him a cross."

"Doesn't need it, not today. So tell me," he asks for the third time, "what are you going to do for them?" And he hands me an unfinished cross. And the knife.

The afternoon was a blur. My people drifted in, his people drifted in; my people came in up, his people left up; my people came in empty and that was good, his people left full and that was good. Around four o'clock one of my women came in, laughing and bleeding. She'd been out six hours giving away Bibles, came back twice for refills. Dog tired, she was returning to church with her bag of leftover Bibles on one shoulder, purse on the other. When she got to the nearby corner, down the street, some young tough knocked her down, grabbed the bag, tore the purse off her shoulder, looked into the purse, looked into the bag, threw the purse down, ran off with the bag.

"Just another Bible thumper, my, my, my." She kept chuckling. Tracy Lee came over, gave her hug, then he knelt down and wiped the blood off her scraped knees. "There, good as new," he said, standing up. "Here," and he put a cross in her purse. I nodded.

He had to work late, his people were coming in, the pace had picked up, mine had slowed down. I had never been so tired.

My subway car on the El was packed so I rode the little platform between the cars. The breeze felt good.

Day Three

On the third day I rose up early, feeling like an earthquake had rattled my bones, shaken me to the core, woke me up out of my twenty year old slumber. At the El I was disappointed not to see Tracy Lee. I walked up and down the platform, checked both entrances, waited through three more train arrivals before finally catching the fourth. The way he works he deserves to sleep late, that was my thought as I turned my attention to my neighbors in their apartments. Twice I waved, once they waved back.

Getting off the El I chose not to duck and weave my way to church. Like an old fashioned gunslinger, I dared them to shoot me.

At the church the door was locked. A boy was sitting on the stoop. Not just any boy, that boy. The almost-murderer. The one whose day it wasn't to kill. And he had the wood plank with the nails; he was practice-swinging, like a baseball player. And no Tracy Lee.

"You him?" he snarled.

"Who?"

"No. You're not him. You're too ..." and his words trailed off. No problem, I could fill in the silence on my own. Yes, I'm too whatever. They would all fit. I'd always been too whatever.

The church door got unlocked by the sexton, the boy followed me in a little too close. No Tracy Lee. The sexton said he had left at 11 p.m. when the last AA meeting had ended. Packed everything in his knapsack and left. "Handed me this cross at the door," which he pulled out of his back pocket. Perfect, polished, smooth.

No Tracy Lee there. Just one boy of uncertain motives, who followed me to my little corner, twirling, if you can believe it, a piece of wood with nails in it.

He sat across from me, like the Bible ladies did each morning, eager, ready, focused. He put the wood plank on the table, nails up. I swear there were blood specks on it, but he was distracted.

"I heard he had something for me," he muttered softly, not threateningly. My little corner was a small table, two chairs, lots of boxes, so he started going through the boxes. Gospel of John, English and Spanish. The Psalms. Proverbs. He opened a box of whole Bibles.

"You want one?" I said, without conviction.

"I got one."

Of course you do, I thought to myself. He rummaged some more and found my personal stuff.

"This must be it." On top of a stack of newspapers I'd left yesterday's cross, the unfinished one. "And I'll need this," he said, grabbing the knife.

No Tracy Lee. Just that boy, and me. Wouldn't you know. I'd known Tracy Lee a lifetime for two days, and he always put you front and center. You were the answer to any question. The missing piece.

Without asking, the boy closed down Tracy Lee's corner, dragged my table to the middle of the room, brought over all the boxes of bibles, set up the chairs.

"Our office," he said, and sat down to whittle.

Jesus at Auschwitz

We agreed to meet at the entrance by the sign.

ARBEIT MACHT FREI.

Work sets you free. Right.

I had never been there but it had a fixed place in my mind. My soul. I have as many Holocaust bona fides as a Swedish kid from Queens born after World War II can have. Holocaust literature came of age about the same time I did. I read Elie Wiesel's *Night*, I saw all of *Shoah* on two consecutive days in an empty theatre, I saw Primo Levi portrayed on Broadway. Throughout my life I could see Auschwitz, Bergen-Belsen, Dachau from some perch, above and at a distance. Like a voyeur. *Schindler's List*, the Holocaust Museum, Anita Schorr. More films, more books. *The Boy in the Striped Pajamas*: a perfect allegory for me, the lure of a death camp beckoning to ... to what, exactly? For the German boy, an adventure, yet more than an adventure, a work of friendship, a Biblical walking of the extra mile. He on one side of the fence, wonderfully naïve, oblivious, with a wide-eyed innocence. A Jewish boy on the other side. They bond, they share, they play. Can you guess on which side? To what end?

Rachel is weeping for her children, mirroring our own Rachels weeping for their grandparents and all their loved ones, all their everyone.

A man gave me his Holocaust library before he died. No fiction this time. Names, statistics, graphs, analyses, cold-hard numbers, history, edicts, measurements, cartoons, propaganda. The slow, methodical, theological, sociological, pathological dance with Evil. Personified.

The number 6,000,000 is imprinted on my heart, like the numbers tattooed on the arms of those "selected" for work – though most did not survive.

So, I did my due diligence, getting ever closer to the flame. Terezin. A sort of minor-league Czech Holocaust Williamsburg historic village. A way station between life and death, not a killing field exactly, more a Potemkin village, set up to pacify the already placid, the lipstick on a pig. It worked. People saw there was nothing to see, so the trains kept rolling, taking cargo to heaven.

I sat on a bunk bed in Terezin and wept, and I wasn't even near the flame.

Today, we meet the flame.

He walks in unnoticed; we embrace as though he knows me. The tourists are busy being tourists. Most folks are silent, caught between respect and fear. Some are already weeping, their tour having started long ago.

"You want to walk around, take the tour?" I ask, not knowing how else to break the ice with Jesus or Auschwitz.

"Not a tour, I was here every day, that's enough. I know every square inch."

"You were here?"

He doesn't answer. But he walks with me. It is a surprisingly small place, unsettlingly ordinary. For something that surely is larger than life, this isn't. Such thoughts keep me safe.

I look around to see if anybody recognizes him. To me he stands out. But people see what they want to see. Like Terezin. So nobody really sees him. There are no knowing looks exchanged, no nods of recognition, no tip of the hat to the Master of the Universe, no niceties.

We're just there.

We are in two different worlds despite being side by side. He had that — what is it called? — that thousand-mile stare. Every block we visit, every room, he's looking far and deep. I am fixated on the near, the minute. The crushed rock in the dirt road that feels like rural Maine. A lone braid in the room of shorn hair. A valise with a familiar name in the room of abandoned suitcases. A pair of spectacles that looks like mine in a mountain of eyeglasses. He seems to see all the hair, every strand. And more than suitcases, or eyeglasses.

We barely talked. From time to time I heard a sort of moan. You know the scripture where Jesus cries out "It is finished"? I've never thought he said that. I think he made a sound of sorts, something anguished and final. That's the sound I hear as we leave one building, turn a corner, confront a new block with new … new what? New horror? New obscenity? New proof of demons? New proof of atheism? I don't know. Something new. A courtyard where prisoners were shot or hung. An adjacent room where they were stripped naked before being shot or hung. A little office where it was decided who got shot or hung. Short of such sudden death were rooms designed for suffocation, or starvation, or torture by standing. Who knew? Then a block for medical experiments.

You turn enough corners, and even without trying you hit the trifecta. The only gas chamber *cum* crematorium still standing. Down the street, the Commandant's house. In between, the gallows from which the Commandant was introduced to his Maker. I smile at this small justice. His thousand-mile stare grows longer. We are not in the same place.

It all hangs in the air. War, history, evil, the chimney's residue from one place to another, one time to another.

I don't know what I expected from today. From him. From Auschwitz. From me. So many layers. The silence between us is not out of respect, it's out of fear of what might be said. But I can't stand it. So finally I push. "You said you were here. You watched? You couldn't stop it? You, more than anyone, should know that the stones cry out." I feel so superior quoting scripture.

He doesn't seem taken aback. But his voice is surprisingly flat as he responds. "I was here. I did not watch. I have done what needed to be done. And yes, stones cry out."

It sounds profound but feels like evasion. I need some admission from him, so I dig. "But what do you say about it? You?" I demand. "This is singular, right? Special. Sorry, I can't think of a strong enough word. There isn't a strong enough word. Only Holocaust. I mean, this is <u>the</u> Holocaust." I don't know if I say it as a question or an allegation.

"What?" he says, "You think the Holocaust is new? The Slaughter of the Innocents is new?" His switch from studied indifference to brusque anger catches me off-guard. Perhaps I'd misunderstood his silence. One moment he's sitting on the stairs to Block 24, leaning back on his elbows, looking for all the world like he's relaxed, here in the epicenter of Hell. The next moment he's pacing the tiny plaza in front of the gas chamber, chastising me for apparently not grasping that today's evil is just the tip of an aeons-old iceberg. I'm offended. I hope he doesn't read minds.

He does. "Here's the truth, and you may not wish to hear it." Staring straight at the crematorium, he shakes me to the core as he says: "All of those people are fine. Better than fine. Really. Trust me."

Pause. Long pause. To catch my breath, and not say something I will regret. Truth is, I believe him, but this just doesn't seem the place for Christian triumphalism. This is the place for Christians to shut up. Or show some anger, fury – that would feel better. Or would it? Oh well, he isn't finished.

"Yes, they're fine. And the ones who did it? The perpetrators? They're in their own private Idaho, and it's a lot different than they expected." His look stops me even before I can think up my objection. "I don't do unto others what they have done unto mine."

God, he even speaks King James when he wants to shut me up. It works. For a while there is a heavy silence. I'm uneasy. I hope to God nobody is listening. The first round of Jews was here to die. The latest round is here to remember. Large numbers of Jewish groups, men in yarmulkes, Hasidic families, two contingents of the Israeli Defense Forces – none of these would like where this conversation is headed. I can tell.

In my own way I try to hush him up, which is not hard. The way to hush him is to not talk to him. In such silence we make our way to the other Auschwitz, Birkenau. *The place of the birch trees.* No longer.

We enter where the trains entered. After a while he sits down, just off the platform, near a cattle car, where the trains emptied their treasure.

The silence hates me so I speak up. "They're fine, the Jews. And the others are some sort of fine, too. They're not slowly twisting on a spit over the lake of fire, or something like that? The Nazis, the Poles, the Ukrainians? Everyone who helped, or turned the other way?"

He adds, "And the Hutus, and the Khmer Rouge, and General Custer, and the Turks. All the guests of the killing fields, and all the hosts, all some sort of fine to varying degrees."

I don't know what I expected, but he's not as distressed as I need him to be. At least "varying degrees" hints at purgatory. Sounds like everybody pays something at Hotel California where this may be Heaven, this may be Hell.

"I know this," I tell him a little too self-righteously, with the sweep of the hand, "this is Hell." Case closed.

All my life, the Holocaust was the "case closed" argument. Late night college bull sessions, Philosophy 101, all the Christopher Hitchens newly-baptized atheists, whenever talk turned to God, or how God could be good, or God's unconditional love, the Holocaust stops all debate. There is a Hell. And anyone who did this needs to go to Hell. And where the Hell was He, anyway?

Turns out Jesus is just as quick with a dismissive retort. "You want a Hell to make you feel better. If everybody pays something, then we're even. What would make this even? Besides, if Hell is God's idea it should make God feel better. It's not about you. You're happy telling people to go to Hell – your boss, the umpire, anybody who annoys you, anybody you disagree with. All the way back to your playground days as a kid. Each of you kids telling the others they were going to Hell, quoting some nun, some relative, some know-it-all authority, cursing each other out. Made me want to quote your eleven-year-old self: '*you kiss your mother with that mouth?*'"

So much to digest here. We're sitting at Auschwitz's death camp, debating Hell, he's quoting my childhood persona like he was there, he claims to have been here, he admits he didn't do anything about it, and he tells me that everybody involved is some sort of fine. And he implies, with that look of his, that I just don't get it.

"*Most* people don't get it," he says, once again inserting himself into my private conversation. "Privacy?" he laughs. "Free will, yes. Privacy, no. I do know; and you don't get it." He pauses to let that sink in, which I don't like – because most of what he's saying I don't *want* sunk in.

"What do you think I am, exactly?" Believe me, he isn't waiting for an answer. I notice he said "What" not "Who." "You call me God, some do, or Son of God. Messiah. Prophet. Chosen One. Most people like me; they sense some sort of close connection between me and, you know, the other One."

"Your Daddy," I interject, deciding to one-up him in Bible knowledge. "Your Father who art in heaven, Abba. You said we could call him Daddy."

Now he lets my words sink in, staring at me intently, clearly hoping I would get through to my own self. The other One. Daddy. Father. Creator. God of everything inside this massive industrial machine of death. Jews, homosexuals, Roma, Nazis, collaborators, the bricks in the chimney, the science behind the gas chamber, the bullets, the organizational genius of planners, God was in it all. Is that a comforting thought? Or an awful thought? Is he conflicted, angry, tormented, guilty?

Suddenly I remember a play I saw on TV, set in a barracks at Auschwitz. The Jews, awaiting their fate, decide to put God on trial. I voted: Guilty.

I knew it, he hears me. "Guilty? Perhaps. But of what? Guilty of loving too much?"

This doesn't seem like a good place for him to get defensive, so I press the advantage. "No. Guilty of not doing enough. Not doing anything. Not doing. You're God, for Chrissake. Sorry. You walk around like you're not part of this. You're the genesis of this, at least in part. The Jews are Christ-killers, remember?! Your Church was complicit. Your people were, literally, instrumental. Your cross was the reason for this." How innocent I sound.

I swear, I see smoke coming out of his ears. Hands trembled, voice quivers. I'd hit a nerve.

"*My* cross. You folks have spent two thousand years describing how awful my crucifixion was. You know nothing about my cross. <u>This</u> is my cross. For me, what went on in Jerusalem, on Calvary, was nothing compared to this. Some torn flesh, raw nerves, a few hours, and on to Easter. This … this….” Somehow he makes a sweeping gesture without moving a muscle.

I wait, but no tears. This is beyond tears.

“You know the Auschwitz Cross?” he asks, triggering some vague memory of nuns erecting a cross outside one of the blocks. “Christians want to baptize Auschwitz,” he continues, more sad than disgusted. “Better to re-Judify the Cross. When I died, there were three Jews hanging on crosses that day. More the day before. More the next week. Non-Jews doing it. Jews doing the dying. Maybe we should have six million crosses all over here. Deny *that*,” he adds with contempt.

He is pressing the palms of his hands together, vigorously. “I *know* awful. I was here, for every damned, blessed minute. Every damned, blessed minute. Every damned, blessed minute.”

I could imagine God wrathful, I could imagine God peaceful. This is closer to home. Visceral. This was a mother who had just lost her child. This was a child who had just lost their mother. This was the wailing you hear after another bomb blast by ISIS or Boko Haram or a drone. This is the sob that comes after all the tears are used up and all you are left with is the upheaval of your world.

He’s looking around, slowly, sometimes with his eyes closed as if to see better.

By now we’ve moved closer to the actual hellhole of Auschwitz-Birkenau, the ruins of the gas chamber and crematoria. The pile of rubble could stand in for shattered dreams the world over. On this day we are surprisingly alone. It is where I feared to be and needed to be. It is where he was tired of being.

"This is the worst that it gets, until it gets worse. The Jews are right to declare Never Again. Precisely because it is *never* Never Again, it is over and over and over again, a blasphemy so clear an infidel can see it." Then a deep breath. "I'm talking too much."

"No," I insisted, "you need to talk, people need to hear from you. This was done in your name." I let that hang, sorry I said it, sorry it was so.

But I press again. "Every damned, blessed minute, you say. It is hard to hear those words in the same sentence about this place. Sure, I know my Holocaust literature. One person gives their bread to another. Someone covers up for a sick person. An adult saves a child. Children paint a wall, adults form an orchestra. A German smiles. Even taken all together there's no blessedness worth mentioning in this damnation."

"You're right. Unless you are the one who is the bread. But you're right. The damned is what was done. The blessed are to whom it was done. No amount of good deeds takes away the damnation of this place. And no amount of evil takes away the blessing of my place."

I feared this moment. I really didn't want to hear about heaven in this place; and I really needed to hear about heaven in this place. Can something be inappropriate, and right on time?

"I can't do anything about this." He says it so matter-of-factly that it sounds vulgar.

Given who he is, what he's supposed to be, what I believe him to be, what half the world has believed to be true; given all the books, armies, empires, riches devoted to him, this is hard to hear. Any sentence coming from his mouth beginning "I can't" destroys the world of faith. I'm not going to sit and quote Bible verses to him, but I can't block them from my head. "I can do all things through Christ … anyone who has faith in me will do what I have been doing, even greater things … I will do whatever you ask in my name … all authority has been given to me in heaven and on earth … you can move mountains."

But we didn't move mountains. And he didn't do squat. Together we sound like Roosevelt, who couldn't bomb the crematorium or the railway because he was too busy elsewhere. And now my companion admits he can't. Do anything. About this. He's about to say something and I am about to be pissed. I don't want to hear any Zen Buddha, Deepak Chopra, Dalai Lama, Paulo Coelho, non-attachment, transcendence Pablum. This is too real. People were gas-showered to death, mass-murdered, baked in ovens, scattered to the wind. This is real.

"This is real," he quotes me. "This is real," he bends over, pounds the ground with his fist; "this is real," standing up, both arms do a sweeping 180 degrees; "this is real," thrusting his fist in the air, then pointing in every direction. "This counts, this matters, this feels, this hurts. I know that. That's what incarnation means, flesh in the game. My flesh in the game. Listen, I know your idea of Hell. How many centuries have you folks piously repeated *'He descended into Hell.'* Well, I didn't have to descend too far. I descended into Bethlehem, into Egypt, into Nazareth and Galilee, into Jerusalem, I found Hell every step of the way. I can't un-Hell this. I can't un-free the will you love so dearly. I can't un-eat the apple. What's done is done. You know good, you know evil. You make choices...."

Now I'm angry, "No, I'm not letting you off the hook, you don't just walk away from this unscathed."

Rage impending; I feel it. "Unscathed!? Unscathed?? You don't know anything about me!" That hurts; he scores, but goes on. "Walk a mile in your own damn shoes, you're not ready for mine. Six million Jews? Six million miles I walked. Six million Chosen People? I chose them. Six million plus gays, gypsies, communists, activists, ists and ists and ists, six million plus. Children. My children. My children." He bellows the last, then softens. *"My children."*

Awkward doesn't really capture it. I'm sitting here believing my beliefs probably more than ever. Those ancient Christians argued vehemently about the true nature of Jesus: fully God; fully man; half God, half man. They ended up with one hundred percent God, one hundred percent man. I'm sitting here with the human part, and he seems even more divine. He has earned his stripes, every one. I'm not going to kick him when he's down.

But I want to know there's some purpose. Some redeeming value. Make sense of it all to some end.

This man, so full of surprises, has another one. He says, "I like that song, *'Sympathy for the Devil.'* There's no brag to it, just fact. Horror by horror, evil by evil, 'I was there,' the devil boasts. So was I. There was no sense. No purpose. No value. Don't be over-impressed by the virtue of suffering. Yes, there are people who rise above it, who learn great lessons, heroes, martyrs, sacrifices that inspire those who don't make the sacrifices. My take is *"my God, my God, why hast thou forsaken me?"* I said that on the cross, remember? Some think I was pointing to a brighter day. Really? You think I don't fully grasp the Holocaust. I don't think *you* grasp the cross. Hell: we've got that figured out and mastered. That's why the Devil gets sympathy. He's good at what he does. I can't do that. I can do heaven."

Surprisingly, that doesn't seem like bullshit.

We come to the infamous Crematorium III. What's not infamous here? Despite Nazi pride in their every effort, they grew shy at the end, tried to obliterate evidence. But this skeleton remains carved into the earth. The train platform leads to the stairs, downstairs to the undressing room, turn right into the showers, twenty minutes later dragged out and up to the crematorium above.

Together we look, each in our own nightmare. Then we wander the well-worn path hugging close to the ruins. Here I break away, to be alone. I don't want to be with him.

By the gas chamber I have the world to myself, I think. Just me, and them. Suddenly, I hear the screaming, I hear it, and moans, louder than moans. I feel it. The horror, the terror, the fear, the despair, I feel it. Oh, how I hurt.

Yet I start to calculate, even while being ripped apart. From the train to selection to undressing room – what, twenty minutes? Maybe an hour? Probably some relief to be off the train, on the platform, outdoors, fresh air.

Some hope, even, to be stripped naked, anticipating clean, freshness, a real toilet, a shower. Yes, a shower.

How soon in the gas showers did they realize? Who realized first? How was that most evil of all truths spoken? Why am I thinking like this, thinking at all?

My senseless thoughts are broken by renewed screams as I stare deep into the pit. It's dawning now, on everyone. The gas. People fighting, climbing, scratching, surviving, all the while it can't be. Bodies climbing over bodies, every man for himself. That's how it's always told, imagined. Maybe so. Maybe not always. Down in the bowels people are swooning in surrender, hugging one another, embracing even themselves. Some are praying. Others fighting for life, precious life, sacred life. Arms and eyes reaching, reaching. Up. Where you are. You.

There's a strong chain blocking my entrance to the abyss. With inhuman strength I stand here twisting it, again and again.

Without thinking I let go, lift my arms slowly, a Tai Chi graceful movement, hands open, arms slowly gliding up my sides ending in two praying hands atop my head. The hands, unguided by me, encircle my head, moving down, down, down. As close as I can get from this side, and not just of the chain.

The gas falls gently over me. We breathe in deeply. Come, Sweet Death, I am surprised to hear me say.

But again I hear screams, hear them, I'm telling you. Don't you? I cover my ears but it does not matter. I still hear. I still see. I see arms raised, boney fingers extended, reaching. I see streaks of blood, the only color of the whole day.

And why? Why in the midst of this truest inferno do I find time to make it about me? Yet I do. In pursuit of knowledge, loud enough to assault heaven, I ask, did they curse? Stop believing? Shout at God? Damn God? Cite verses? The Kaddish? And then, with inevitable self-centeredness, I demand *what would I do?* Would I remain faithful? Would I go happily singing hymns to my glorious martyrdom on the way to sainthood?

No, I almost snarl.

No, I declare to the One who swears He was there. As sure as I hear those screams, as sure as I see that blood, as sure as I witness the swoon and embrace, just as sure I know I would have lifted my head up to heaven, to You, O God. I would have cursed you. I would have loved you to the end, believed in you to the end. With my dying breath I would have worshipped. But in the breath before I would have cursed you. For being as helpless as I. As human. And this is not a good place for humans.

At that I choose to look directly into the sun, through the sun, until it hurts, until I can see no more. And I dare God to look at me. I gasp. I sigh. I cry.

Later, I head down the platform path, ignoring some people who whisper as I walk by. Soon he is by my side.

"Remember James Foley?"

"The journalist, beheaded by ISIS?"

"Yes, maybe the first to get everybody's attention. Evil always has to announce itself, even though it never has an off day. So they made a show of James. Evil has such an ego."

"You're telling me James Foley is with you. And I should take some comfort in that, right? After all he went through, capture, betrayal, torture, brutality, humiliation, slaughter, he's one of the ones that's fine now."

"It gets better. Or worse. You know that ISIS fellow who beheaded James Foley?"

I know I'm not going to like this. I just know.

"He's with me. They're both with me. James is not surprised. He loved me all along, counted on me in the darkest corner of his life. In that very moment. I don't know if it was innate, or how he was raised, but it was strong enough to carry him here. Truth is, he's kind of pleased, like 'we won!' – but not in a gloating way. Just very satisfied."

While I take a deep breath, he's breaking one of the inviolate laws of the universe. You know the one: bad guys gotta pay. That's what eternity is for. Payback.

"And?" I ask, looking for clarity but fairly confident I won't like it.

"The other fellow? It's not the heaven he expected, it's not the Hell you expected. He's with me. And James. Sticks pretty close. They're here today...." He trails off.

I'm not filling in any blanks for him here. This is all on him.

"He cries, all the time. Every day. Sometimes he stops, looks around, has one of those gasping sobs that come after all the tears are used up and all you are left with is the upheaval of your world. And then he weeps. He sits by himself, wipes his tears with the corner of his burqa."

"James Foley's murderer wears a burqa?!"

"He doesn't want anyone to recognize him. He's afraid to see his mother."

"Is he the only one in a burqa?"

"There are others weeping, but he's the only one in a burqa. He wears it around, only takes it off in Sunday School. James is his Sunday School teacher."

There are so many thoughts bouncing around my head, but I don't trust myself to scream most of them at him.

For my own benefit I summarize out loud, "You have Sunday School in heaven. The ISIS murderer attends. Foley is the teacher."

He doesn't acknowledge my sarcastic disgust.

"Well, some people like it. Some use it as a refresher course, some never got it in the first place. It's remedial, A.P., Life-Long Learning all rolled into one," Jesus explains, as if it makes sense.

Suddenly, I hate to admit it, but I soften. Maybe my hatred hurts too much. Maybe I need to believe. Memories come back of all those Sunday School Bible stories, told with a flannel-graph or a filmstrip projector: Jesus with a little sheep around his shoulders, blessing children, walking around a hot but happy Middle East. It seemed possible then. Maybe. Somehow. If. A breath of fresh air in the Hell of my own soul.

"Once he asked me for Hell. You're not the only types who want a real, fire-breathing Hell. Some folks think they deserve it. It almost seems preferable, some ways easier, than...."

Here he has a catch in his throat, like men get when they are emotional but don't want to show it. I finish his sentence. "Love."

"Yeah, love. People think it's so easy, they slough it off like some lesser thing. They think all the other stuff is harder: anger, war, vengeance, hatred, punishment. People don't know."

Dead silence. He's spent, an *it is finished* kind of spent.

"I know the feel of the blade on the neck. I know the feel of the hand on the blade as it slid across the neck."

And then he sobs. Big, heaving, silent, empty sobs. And still, no one sees him. Maybe some work sets us free.

Water Into Wine

A Long Sunday

The first priest knew I was a fake
the second smiled for Christ's sake
the third, too young to care,
just proud I was there.
The first priest drank all the wine
the second gave me a long sip
the third, too young to share,
I caught taking a nip.
The first priest had tradition
the second had Christ
the third would one day
grasp sacrifice.

I turned water into wine. Why? Because I was asked.

Legend has it that in every Philosophy department of every liberal arts college there was an exam with one question: Why?

Legend has it that the only student to ace the exam used his classic, blue exam booklet to answer, "Why not?"

More mundane parallels, perhaps apocryphal, have the bank robber answering why he robs banks with, "Because that's where the money is." And the mountain climber, explaining his risky passion for mountains with,

"Because they're there." Or Freud, who said, "Sometimes a cigar is just a cigar."

Why do people want deep, complex, oblique, shrouded-in-mystery puzzles, something to ponder? When sometimes the obvious says it all.

I turned water into wine. Why? Because I was asked.

I heard a preacher twist himself in knots to explain this breach of Georgia Baptist protocol, proclaiming, "It was unfermented grape juice." Sure. An Israeli wedding ran out of Kosher Chianti and I replaced it with Welch's grape juice, and everybody was happy. Please. I'm at a village wedding. Take it at face value. Sometimes a cigar is just a cigar, and wine is, well, wine.

A wedding day, for the two families joining together, is the culmination of lifelong dreams, a little maternal plotting around the village well, some divine intervention. For the two kids, this really is the biggest day of their lives, not just of their young lives but of their whole lives. They are King and Queen for a day. I've been to weddings where crowns are put on the couple's heads, and they sit on thrones. And for little Cana it really was a big deal.

This was not a wedding where the mother of the bride sits down with a budget, comes up with a guest list acceptable to both families, pares it down to size, picks out a venue twelve months in advance, does a tasting, books the church, then starts worrying about the big issues: wedding dress and color scheme.

This was bigger. Cana might be nowhere to you. But to them it was the center of the universe. And on this wedding day the universe watched. First, everybody was invited. Second, everybody came. There was nothing else going on. There was no Cana Little League, no Cana Country Club, no Cana Theatre, no Cana Walmart on the edge of town. Nothing to distract anyone. No iPhones to put down, TV to turn off, shopping to do. That day was wedding day all day for everyone.

I didn't want to go. My mother made me. Jesus, that's embarrassing to say, but it's true.

And I'm allowed to say "Jesus," right? I know I'm not to take the Lord's name in vain, but it is my name. You are still getting used to the idea that I made sure everyone had plenty of wine, and now I've broken the Third Commandment. I apologize.

But yes, my mother made me go. Like the cigar just being a cigar, sometimes a son is just a son, and every son knows that, and every mother reminds every son of that. You don't have to be a mama's boy all the time to be a mama's boy some of the time.

You wonder about our family dynamics? If *dysfunctional* describes a family that does not function in expected ways then your Holy Family was dysfunctional.

Our functionality, our family dynamic, let's face it, is the result of – ta-da – "The Virgin Birth." What? You don't believe in the Virgin Birth?! Well, my parents believed it, and that is how they functioned. In our house, something magical happened, not on Christmas Eve, but way before. A miracle, a mystery, a God-ordained, God-begun gestation that brought me into being. I know the words you folks toss around at Christmas. Incarnation: God made flesh. Emmanuel: God with us. Virgin Birth: my Dad on the sidelines.

Do I believe it? There isn't a kid anywhere who wants to imagine his parents' sex life, or lack of it. You just don't go there. That makes for a lot of immaculate conceptions. But I'm humoring you. You want to know if I believe in the honest to goodness Virgin Birth, that God's spirit took over the biology of my mother and gave life to someone fully God and fully human – me?

Yes, I believe it. All my life a mist hung over our family. I don't want to use words like cloud or shroud, you'll read too much into that, and this whole story is about reading too much into something. There was an aura around our family. Is that too New Agey for you? Or Old Agey? No, we didn't walk around with halos over us like the medieval paintings have it. It is something we felt. Not so much a covering as a hovering. Add to that the hints and whispers and what I heard and overheard, and I got the picture. Believe me, when my mother told me, "Your father wants you to _____" or "Your father wouldn't be happy about _____," I knew which one was Joseph and which wasn't. It was intuition. We never had a family conference, with Joseph clearing his throat and, with gravitas, saying, "We need to talk, son. No, not about that; well, maybe it is, a little bit, but that's not the point. How about if I begin at the beginning, and you don't interrupt."

I didn't interrupt because we never had the talk. We had stories. Your basic Sunday School Christmas Pageant, minus the chronology and the drama. Just stories. This one about shepherds. That one about Wise Men. Another about Bethlehem.

One day some friends and I were playing soldier, and one of the older boys started slashing the air with his stick sword – pretending to be Herod's soldiers killing the babies in Bethlehem, he bragged. Other kids provided background noise, stomping feet, shouts, screams, groans, orders, wailing.

That night, when I told my parents, they got very silent for a very long time. Finally, my mother said, "Yes, we had a bad king. Eat. You need your strength." The same thing she always said to change the subject if the stories started to add up. Star over Bethlehem. Gee, the weather is good for the crops this year. My behavior on a family trip to Jerusalem. New order for furniture for the carpentry shop. Crucifixions are up this year. The fish are biting in Galilee. The Rabbi said the Messiah is coming. Spring is coming. Stories to interrupt stories.

The wine, yes, back to the wine. Holy Family not-withstanding, halo-effect, miracle-talk, God-inordinately-close notwithstanding, we were still mother and son. And mother was invited to the wedding, I never caught why, relative of a relative, I was told. Let's face it, on a wedding day everybody is a cousin.

Why I was dragged along probably has to do with a mother's pride. In my mind I was a nobody, but on the verge of something. If you promise not to misunderstand, it seems I was on the verge of being a Holy Man, a prophet, a guru, if you will. Some called me "Rabbi," which means teacher. I like that. Teacher. People definitely did listen to me, I had a following. It is uncomfortable for me to talk that way, but I'm trying to give you an idea of how I ended up in Cana.

My mother had married a country carpenter, now her son has become a popular religious figure. People hang on his every word, he's a topic of conversations, a person of interest, an object of gossip. I was a boldface name in a small town newspaper, and my mother was going to present me. It was a command performance. She commanded, I performed. It felt that way even before the wine.

The wedding was wonderful. The bride was lovely, the groom was proud, the tent was packed, the food was bountiful, people were happy, and I was unobtrusive. Like clergy at every wedding reception, everybody wants us there, but nobody really wants us there. We might dampen the festivities. I tried hard not to dampen. I and my entourage of disciples sat at a far table, talking amongst ourselves, family stuff, a little politics, jokes about Romans, nothing worth repeating.

Up front I noticed a flurry of activity, the parents in animated conversation, furrowed brows, one telling another to keep it down. Somehow my mother is over there and I know, this can't be good. My mother has this way of being in other people's business. She could be the patron saint of other people's business. Which, in a way, she is.

Summoning me, she drops it all in my lap. "They're out of wine," she says matter-of-factly.

I blanked. That's my only defense for what I said to her, I just blanked. I was rude. You can harden it, you can soften it, nothing fixes it.

There are three things in my life I regret, that I'll tell you about. Snapping at my mother. Later on, calling a foreign woman a dog. And at the end, cursing a fig tree. All three inexcusable. As they teach young soldiers when they mess up, the only response is, "No excuse, sir." Amen.

To reset the table: big wedding, happy day, wine runs out, my mother expects me to fix it. Without thinking (God, I hope so) I blurt out, "Why involve me? My time has not yet come."

In the Bible, printed on the fancy paper with classic font, my words sound innocuous, almost holy. "Dear, dear Mother," I might be saying, "I must save the world, no trivialities for me." To make it more contemporary, "Mom, don't waste my time." To preach it out, "Mother, you have known God's plan from the beginning. I am headed to the cross for the sins of the world. This work has started, I've gathered a few disciples, we're rolling it out in stages. I'm not ready yet to show my hand." Or on the street, "Fuhgeddaboutit." All versions of "Don't bother me. It's not my time."

I'm glad my father wasn't there, either one, they'd have slapped my face and washed my mouth out with soap.

My mother, however, didn't miss a beat. She didn't feign hurt or take umbrage; she coolly turned to the servants and said, "Do whatever he tells you to do."

Maybe it wasn't my time. Maybe it was her time. Or the couple's time. And the village's time. All I know is that my mother was ready, and maybe she did know God's time better than I.

The rest of the story is fairly famous, and mostly misses the point. There's some stone jars nearby, I tell the servants to fill them with water. The maître d' of the wedding tastes it, he's so impressed he grabs the groom in a proud embrace and offers this social commentary: "Most folks serve the good stuff early in the reception; once everyone is feeling too good to notice they start serving the cheap stuff. But you, my boy, are the class of Cana. You have saved the best for last."

At that point my disciples are really proud to be with me. Because, when I called them to be my disciples I was rather blunt. I told them foxes have holes, birds have nests, but I have nothing to offer you, nowhere to even lay my head. Now we are the stars of a banquet, with our own winery. Things are looking up.

Later, my mother caught my eye, nodded her head ever so subtly, with the hint of a smile. Not smug. Knowing. Very, very knowing.

Of course, everyone insisted we stay the night, treated us like royalty the next morning before we hit the road.

Demons, lepers, fig trees awaited. If Constantine really did see a cross leading to victory, I believe it. I saw it, too.

Did I answer your "why" about the wine? Well, this is one of those cigars that is just a cigar. My mother asked. And the kids needed it. Don't read too much into it, needs versus wants. Two people in love, everybody that matters to them is there, they want the night to last. They're not worried about who's driving the donkey home, or if Uncle Harry's had too much. It seemed a small thing, a nicety, a gesture. Call it a wedding gift. More came later.

The Communion of Saints

I drove up to Maine looking for some roots. We come from there, back in the day, before we got citified, urbanized, secularized, bastardized, and worse words used for those who live a little bit east of Eden, right up next to Sodom, not far from Gomorrah.

Driven there by a dream, one I couldn't shake loose in the morning and seemed fed by the daylight. Came with instructions, a divine GPS. Who knew.

I found those familiar back roads I had never been on, took the correct turns and ended up home in places I had never been.

The house I came upon was regal in its bare simplicity. Everything bespoke home, eternity, labor, pride, humility. Yes, the last two can go together. Proud of who you are, humble with how you are.

I parked under a tree that must have inspired Joyce Kilmer, but he was from New Jersey. Walking up the driveway bits of sun fell through the trees like a blessing.

I could smell the garden growing, and laundry hanging on the line waved me toward the back. "Get thee to a far country," God had said to Abraham, pointing toward a Promised Land. And an old man.

When I found him he was sawing out in the back forty. That's a joke, he said, they didn't have but a front yard and a back yard, enough for old stuff to rust and vegetables to grow. To me it looked like Iowa, but I've never been to Iowa.

Without introductions, as if I had caught him mid-sermon rather than mid-sawing, I wasn't even sure if he was talking to me, but he says, "The thing about faith is, some things you know, and some things you believe. Some things you need to believe, some things you want to believe, some things you got to believe, some things you reach to believe."

This was the whitest old man I had ever seen but in the middle of nowhere Maine he had the cadence, and the hard, sharp-edged, "huh" of those old time black preachers I heard on my travels. Roots run deep, and spread out.

People dropped by as if expected. To borrow from the shed, to listen, to see this strange thing that has happened, someone quoted Biblically. About me, it seems. It was all of an afternoon, the ebb and flow of stories and people.

In the timeless hours ahead people knew me, or the smell of me, familiar hayfields and apple orchards and slate quarry. Stranger or long-lost relative, each one greeted me in the offhand manner of someone long awaited and not surprised to see me. On the porch, in the front yard, behind the screen door, back of the barn, chopping wood, at the oven, on the tractor, near the church, a whole Thornton Wilder cast of characters no more in the cemetery here than there, just as alive as when they knew me.

Conversations got started mid-thought as though my arrival was no interruption, my presence seamless with what had long been said and was still to be heard. I wasn't even a comma.

The old man really was Everyman, Maine version. What L.L. Bean makes you think, not look. Everything broken in, skin, clothes, tools, voice, ideas, him.

He did most of the talking, others joined in as I moved about, all of a whole even with what didn't agree. What was agreeable was us, and everything fit in or didn't matter.

"This lady I know, nice lady, she's just determined to believe that a man should not lay with another man; Jesus never said anything about it, but she holds to that belief."

He didn't look to me for confirmation, but he said the name Jesus like he knew him, quite well, and put a lot of stock in him. He's still sawing, one of those old men who work up a sweat and still don't look like they're sweating. It's like breathing. He knows the saw, and hard work, like he knows Jesus, first name basis, quality time together.

"I know this other lady, she told me flat out that God gave her cancer as a personal gift just for her, like God picked her out the way they pick someone out of the audience on a TV show, "Come right up here, young lady, have I got a surprise for you,' and He gives her cancer because...."

And here the old man stops sawing, straightens up and appears to be quoting God directly as spoken to this other lady. "Because I know you can handle it, others might waste it, but you can use it for my glory."

I don't know what to say about either lady, but it's clear the old man isn't testing me. He's talking with me like talking with me is important enough. He stretches his back like a great hitter does before he steps up to the plate, something he did a lot of back in his day. They say he was good, the pros had an eye on him, but God got him.

Before he bent back to work, he shrugged, one of those shrugs that up there says about five pages of dialogue, including more than a few opinions. His audience was appreciative.

"Faith is a funny thing," he says, then goes into the exact same speech he gave before, but not like it was a riff he pulled every time a stranger dropped in, but like it was something he knew, not just believed.

One of his sons walked up, nodded at me in a friendly way, started picking up the wood planks. And in harmony with the old man he moved into the conversation the same way a brook moves into the Androscoggin, right at home. "And there was that farmer up in Monson, his tractor fell right over on top of him. Lay there to die. His son came home, went looking for his Daddy, found him under that tractor, picked it up and tossed it aside like a sack of potatoes, saved his Daddy's life. Next morning he tried to right that tractor and couldn't budge it, not an inch."

The son, like the old man, talked and worked without stopping, or looking at you, or sweating. Stories just rolled out, you could weigh them on your own but they were told as Gospel truth, make of it what you will.

He told about the Deacon's wife, full of cancer, doctors had given up, she went to a Tent Revival Meeting with Oral Roberts. Came home cured. Said so by the doctor.

The old man told about the drunkard, heard Billy Graham preach, got saved that night, never touched a drop since, went back to his wife, his children, his work, made himself a good life.

He told about the town's own "Good Thief," found a Bible in a hotel room, opened it up blind, right to the part about the thief on the cross who asked Jesus to remember him. The town thief came home, went down to his basement, found everything he had ever took, started going around town late at night, leaving things on people's porches.

The son would tell a story, the old man would do that deep-throated "huh"; the old man would tell a story, the son would nod at his father with a "yessir," back and forth, like a tennis match of salvation.

The day was getting long, neighbors drifted home, wood fires were burning all around. The old man's wife made sure I stayed for dinner. Some of it came straight from the garden, the cucumbers with vinegar and black pepper, the carrots with dirt still on them. The rest came from a woodstove even older than the old man and his wife.

Before we ate, the wife had us all take hands and she gave a bottomless prayer that touched upon all of life, with gratitude and beseeching. Jesus was no unseen guest at this meal. He was there, and at home.

They asked about me but seemed to know enough already. I could give them biography and credentials and cite accomplishments but I had already earned my place at the table. I was there. What felt like some mystical bond was, for them, daily life.

"The thing about faith is, some things you know, and some things you believe. Your grandfather...."

My grandfather. He had been in my dream, but the dream was like a photo album with all the pictures out of order. When I arrived they gave no special recognition to my name, and I hadn't yet thought to mention him. I arrived. I entered into what they were doing. Now we were eating a dinner straight out of 1805. As I imagined baked beans out of an earthen pot, out they came.

"Your grandfather, he was some preacher. He preached about heaven and hell in such a way that when church ended some couldn't wait to rush outside to see if Jesus had come, and some lingered inside afraid that maybe he had. As a boy he had looked the Devil in the eye, and gave him his comeuppance. He was a man who knew."

The old man and his wife were sitting there like that old farmer couple in the painting, except instead of farming equipment they each had a fork and knife in their hands. Not menacing, just emphatic. The boy kept eating. We all returned to sawing the pork chops.

I have had two periods in my academic life. For the first twenty years I wanted to sit far back, in a corner, behind a big classmate, slouched over, hoping never to be called upon. Studied indifference masking studied ignorance. Then, quite suddenly, I rushed to get to class early, I wanted a front row seat to be in the best position to ask questions. It now dawns on me that the change came when I changed. This old man would probably call it something equally old, like born again, washed in the blood, got saved, seen the light, hit the sawdust trail, been redeemed, conversion. That's all fine and good, but all I know is I called. God answered. I went from trying hard to know nothing, to wondering about everything.

But now, sitting at my American Gothic supper table, I am back to hiding in a corner, not wanting to show my ignorance, afraid to sound foolish. I say nothing. The conversation around me bounces ever so naturally from the supernatural to the mundane. Someone had a baby. Someone had a message from God to deliver on Sunday in Church. The old folks' home is hiring. The preacher said no to the lady with the message from God. A logging truck turned over on the main road. The lady is starting a new church so she can give her message.

The old man sopped up the leftovers on his plate with a piece of bread, ate with satisfaction. He cleared his throat and said, "I was a preacher, round and about; my own church, once." His wife gave him a "hush, now" scowl, but he was already revved up. "The people always wanted to know about the Devil. Devils and demons and such. Someone was always being taken by the Devil, carried away by the Devil, led astray by the Devil, all going to the Lake of Fire. One Sunday I told them to go slow on filling that Lake. There's always somebody says so and so's in the clutches of the Devil. Wants me to stand him up, right there in church, condemn him. I say, OK. But it should make some difference whether so and so took the Devil's hand, or if his arm got twisted up behind his back. Oh, I'll say there was some commotion. I'm getting modern, they said, wishy washy, no backbone. That didn't sit well with me. We parted company."

He took a slow sip of hot water, looked at his hands. "It wasn't perfect, not my preaching, not my church. But I surely did take it to heart. It was your grandfather's idea."

We moved to the sitting room for a short while. The old man now relished telling stories of my grandfather – and then, to my surprise, mentioned my father.

"You knew my father?" A silly question. He knew my grandfather, he lived his whole life in this old town, in this old house, near that old river. Of course he knew my father. Now he told me of their exploits, he and my father, often done together, rambunctious, faintly rebellious, occasionally dangerous. They both lived to laugh and love another day, I was assured with a wonderful twinkle. And they both did their darndest to be useful for the Lord, that was the meat of it, he emphasized, the meat of it, this said quite earnestly.

Too soon, the old lady called to me from upstairs, my room was ready. They hadn't spoken of it, I didn't want to, but it was all a given. It seemed like being on one of those airport moving sidewalks in the middle of Maine with gates for Norway, Paris, Poland Springs, and you couldn't get off until the end. So I went upstairs at 9 p.m. to a feather bed with feather pillows under a feather quilt. I sneezed all night, and slept deep.

Morning came early. So did breakfast. Whatever I imagined a farmer's breakfast to be, this topped it. All I had done yesterday was listen, eat, and watch others work, but I was famished. Half way through, the other son showed up with his wife and kids, we all spread out around the table, passing and forking, reaching and pouring, and always thanking.

"Some things you know. Some things you believe. Maybe because you need to, or want to, or got to, or you are reaching to. Faith is all of that."

I was startled by the sudden return to yesterday's recurring theme, and the subtle absence of word-for-word cadence. "People don't fight over what they know. They fight over what they believe. You know something, you don't argue about it; someone else doesn't know it, that's their loss. You done your best just telling it. But when you only believe something, you don't want somebody questioning because you're not so sure yourself. You're on shaky ground already, you don't need somebody jumping up and down shaking you up more. You want some 'amen.'"

"Amen," said the new brother, but I couldn't tell if he was joshing with the old man, or agreeing. Still, it was an "Amen."

"Your grandfather knew. I saw him once at the Camp Meeting grounds, sitting outside the Tabernacle on a wood stump. He had his Bible on his lap, but wasn't reading, he's just staring off in the distance. I asked him, quietly, what was he thinking about? He says, 'Heaven. What else is there?' He knew heaven. It was a place. It was peopled. He was going. It was good. He knew. That's how he could preach so powerfully. He preached what he knew. Some preachers, they shout because they're preaching what they think, trying to shout your unbelief down. But when you know you don't shout. Your grandfather knew."

I knew my grandfather as an old man. Old, grizzled, with that faraway look. I didn't know him as a young man, or a carpenter, or a preacher who didn't shout, or a fighter or a ballplayer. But I did know the faraway look.

"He believed in hell," the old wife added. I wasn't sure if she was adding the belief for emphasis, or the hell. Both worked.

"So do I," the old man replied, surprisingly with a smile. Not a happy-about-hell smile; a happy-that-the-battle-is-engaged smile. Life is breath, and breath is for talking, and talking is, well, for this old man, life.

"I know hell isn't popular, and I don't know the ins and outs of it, and I don't like the idea of Peter sitting at the Pearly Gates picking and choosing. But I look at this world full of troubles, and some folks must have to pay, somehow, some way. It's not up to me, I'm just saying some folks need a reckoning. I'll leave it at that."

The new son has been doing triple duty, feeding the youngest child, whispering with his mother, and listening intently. "In our church we go easy on hell," he adds, smiling at us all.

Another stereotype out the window. I figured these were likable, salt of the earth folks who attended a local, independent, fundamentalist church in a mobile home outside of town, having split in a snit from every other church in town. Instead, this son tells me they all go to the congregational church on Main Street. The old man explained, "Our grandkids love the Sunday School, the folks are real nice, the preacher is pretty. And I'll give her this. She knows Jesus."

For once the old man is looking at me with a smile that says only one thing. "Gotcha."

"People think I'm a crazy, old coot. I'm just an old coot with some crazy notions. Like Martians." In one fell swoop the fertilizer hit the fan, bringing out a host of *now there there*, hand grabbing, eye-rolling, *take the kids outdoors, may I have some more coffee, those pancakes were the best*, all efforts to stop a lovely chance encounter with a lost relative from going off the rails.

Sheepishly, I veered off the rails, too. "The Martians, well, sir, the Martians were in my dream. The dream. The one that persisted even after I woke up, and even continued. That led me to come here. There was an old man, sawing wood, he was talking about heaven, and Martians. No reason, he just seemed to care about them." I swear I heard that hard "huh", a "harrumph" and an "Amen" all at once, and some tongue clicking like my mother used to do. And if you can hear an eye roll, I heard that, too, all around the table.

Maybe it was time to leave. Maybe the sons would show me to the front door. Maybe the old man and I need to see a therapist.

"Let's go downtown," one of the sons suggested. Happily, after that hearty breakfast, we walked. Nothing is too far in this town. The whole family and I, an untidy parade, crossed a little bridge, over the falls that used to fuel the mill, toward a tiny church. Ramshackle, well-worn. We walked in through an unlocked side door. Memories of a place I had never been to made it feel like home. The kids spread out on the pews with their Matchbox cars, revving and racing. The women sat side by side, keenly observing.

The old man took charge, full of remembering. "Your grandfather stood up there," he said, pointing to an ornate, brown wood pulpit with velvet covering, "a giant of a man." All 5'4" of him, I smiled to myself. "A giant of a man. He loved harder, loved stronger, loved longer than anyone could know. He loved a lot of tough wood into heaven, a lot of tough wood. I don't know about hell, but he knew heaven."

Both boys had their arms around the old man who had that great stiff upper lip, quivering just enough to pull down a tear. He wasn't embarrassed. "Tears and sweat are the same stuff," he said to no one in particular, or to all of us. "Tears and sweat make a man."

I went up to the pulpit, trying to imagine a life spent behind it. It didn't seem a pulpit made for pounding. If our religion is good news this felt like a good place to learn it.

The old man walked over to the first pew, sat down, then sort of stretched out comfortably, each hand caressing the wood. "Your Dad and I sat right here."

This was all coming at me from so many directions, on so many levels. Family I didn't know but who knew me. Dreams I couldn't understand but I was living them. A past that was very present. And Martians.

"We used to talk about Martians, your Dad and me. Outer space was big in those days. Buck Rogers, H.G. Wells. One Saturday afternoon we snuck into a real movie theatre to see Flash Gordon. And we had our own thinking, too. It wasn't that odd. Your grandfather would often be up there in that pulpit preaching from Daniel and Revelation." My blank stare did not offend him. He went on, "He'd talk about angels and heaven, about Jesus coming back on a white horse, about a whole world that was out there, up there, yet very, very real right here," and he tapped the pew emphatically. "One Wednesday night service, we thought we were in trouble. Baseball went late, we got to church late, and your Dad was the piano player. During hymn requests I raised my hand to show my attention, and I requested, 'O Beulah Land.' Then there was a Bible reading, about meeting Jesus in the air. When we settled in for the sermon, I drew some Martians on the inside cover of the hymnbook. Your Dad leaned over and made some additions. We had a story going. Your grandfather watched it all, kept preaching, never missed a beat. After church we figured we were in for it, especially when everyone left and he sat down on the pew with us. Opened the hymnbook right to our drawings. Hmm, hmm, I heard him say. Hmm, hmm."

I looked around. Every single one of us – sons, wives, grandchildren, me – we were an attentive audience. Something was going on here. Maybe special, maybe beautiful, maybe weird, maybe all three. But it wasn't just an old man telling old stories.

The old man was quiet, until a grandchild prodded him. "Was he angry at you, grandpa? For writing in the book?"

The old man picked up a hymnbook, opened it up, flipping the pages, maybe hoping to find his story. "No, he wasn't angry. He was a serious man, not given to laughter, but there was a smile to his eye that evening. He says to us, 'Nephtali.' 'Seraphim,' your Dad says back. 'Martians,' your grandfather said. We were surprised. No question mark. He just said it. 'Martians.' Your Dad and I looked at each other. Puzzled. We weren't afraid, not quite. Your grandfather wasn't one to hit, no belt buckle. He lectured. He would talk you to death 'til you wanted the belt. We felt a lecture coming on.

Your grandfather shut the hymnbook, went to the pulpit to fetch his Bible, opened it and spoke it to us without looking at the page. 'I have other sheep you know not of,' he told us. Then he came back down to our pew, we gathered up our baseball equipment, he put an arm around each of us, and we walked out. No lecture."

We were all still. However those words hung in the air for the old man decades ago, they stared us in the face right then and there. Other sheep.

One son broke the silence. "I always thought 'other sheep' meant the Catholics, then when I married one I discovered they thought 'other sheep' meant us! And maybe a good Buddhist."

I was so deep inside my own head that I missed some of the good humor going about in our little group, talking about this exclusion and that inclusion and surprising linkages in a world more aware of other sheep.

"Let's go in the other room," the other son said, "you should see something."

We left the sanctuary through the door next to the little choir loft, into their fellowship hall. It was easy to imagine pot-luck suppers, coffee hours, rummage sales, Sunday School taking place here. The old man walked straight to the far wall, moved aside an old poster to reveal a bronze plaque. It seemed forgotten now but once, I'm sure, a place of honor.

It had my grandfather's full name, and below it two words: Psalm 1, like everyone would know it by heart. "It's the Psalm of a Good Man," the old man told me, guessing I was out of my element when it came to memory verses. "He was a good man."

As we started to leave, the old man replaced the poster over the plaque, a faded flyer for a showing of the Left Behind movie. Some people get whisked off to heaven, most are left behind to suffer. The old man looked at it, thoughtfully, and took it down.

"Martians," he chuckled to himself, remembering more than he let on.

That afternoon I said my goodbyes to a family I never knew, and they said goodbye as if I never left. Memories and tastes lingered and multiplied as I did my own little private tour of our sacred spaces. At the Camp Meeting grounds that gave shape to so much, ringed by white birch and green pine, I heard a piano. At the old town team baseball field I squatted behind home plate, stood in the batter's box, made a leap at first base, sat in the dugout. I heard cheering. At the paper mill, long since abandoned, I smelled sawdust and heard the lumber being cut, saw my grandfather in the corner, reading his Bible.

Just like the dream.

The Prodigal's Mother

"Brats."

Jesus actually used that word. "The Kingdom of God is for brats," he said, emphasizing *brats* even louder than Kingdom. Then, not so subtly indicating my son with a nod of the head, he added "and it looks like the Kingdom of God is at hand!"

Thus begins my story of resurrection.

The dead alive. Can you believe it? In our world, a little village, really, death is very personal, always close at hand. We die where we live. The house or the field, that's it. The occasional prodigal runs off to a faraway place, most never seen again, dead or alive. Around here we die where we sit, or lie, or fall.

No one is alone in life or death. We are not just neighbors by proximity. We are family, clan, tribe, religion. The lesson of Cain rings loud: we are our brother's keeper, in life and in death.

When death comes, we hear it, share it, smell it, deal with it. The whole village gathers, work stops, we stare, we linger. We don't turn away. The body is touched, embraced, washed, prepared, wrapped, accompanied, buried deep. All that makes for life is absent. The dead are done and gone to whatever our holy men tell us is next. But it is not life here.

And so, to talk about the dead returning to life is no small matter. It betrays our experience. It confuses our religion. It challenges our understanding of life itself. Yet I must speak of it.

It begins with my son. When I tell you the story of his resurrection you will dismiss it as a mother's embroidery, a parable of sorts, not a real death breathed back to life. But we lived it, the death and the resurrection. And, there is no doubt, it was Jesus whose breath returned us all to life.

Jesus was here twice. Some say the dead go to a hell, a Sheol, a Gehenna. He came first into our hell. Some say the dead go to a paradise, the world as God intended. He came second to our paradise.

Then he headed toward his own hell. We knew it. There was already talk about him, good and bad. The good seemed obvious to us, but the bad seemed obvious to others. And the others had more power. Whether it was destiny that marked him, or ill will, who I am to know?

When, later, he was crucified, we grieved as for one of our own, but we were not surprised. And when, some days after, word reached us that Jesus was alive, I was not surprised. He has the gift of life.

Because of that life, the things that he said and did are of great importance. People are even asking me what he did here. Well then, let me tell the story of our family, my sons, that one son in particular. And Jesus. Others may learn from us.

The first time Jesus came to us was on the worst day of our lives. He showed up out of thin air and entered into our hell. People, then, didn't know what to make of him. Some said he must be Elijah, or one of the other prophets, sent back for who-knows-what. He walked on water, I'm told. I wouldn't bet against that. But he came to us as our Emmanuel, God-with-us. Yes, I know the word.

Let me be clear. My son was trying to destroy our family. He came close. Somehow Jesus took control of us, in a gentle but firm way. Our whole hell hadn't happened overnight. Neither did the healing. The pain was excruciating. We made mistakes along the way. But Jesus taught us a love beyond anything we could imagine. He listened to our woes, advising us to be patient, turn the other cheek, don't close the door. He told us to forgive our son 490 times. I didn't know if he was joking, or actually keeping count, but since he didn't have any kids I let him know my count.

"We're way over that," I told him. "Seventy times seven, plus quite a few you don't know about. They add up."

"I can imagine."

"No, you can't."

"Yes. I can."

Watching Jesus at work is watching a miracle unfold without knowing it is a miracle. He approaches everything with a serenity that is not just calming but – what is that old word? – fetching. Yes. His serenity is fetching, attractive, catchy. Nothing fazes him. Each challenge is met as though the outcome will be right.

They say that in his own village a crowd wanted to kill him, but he walked right through the middle as if they were friends. He talked to Lazarus like he was alive, while Lazarus was dead. He sees beyond the worst of the day.

People say he even quiets storms. This I know. Our house was a storm and that son was a first-class hurricane. Until Jesus entered. That began a miracle equal of – well, resurrection. When Jesus came the second time and saw the miracle of our son returned to our family, perhaps we were the proof he needed to go forward. Perhaps we were a blessing to him.

Now no resurrection surprises me.

I shall always treasure seeing Jesus in our front yard, on that second visit, and remembering my son walking over to us with that familiar attitude in his walk, he's always had it. Some things don't change, and that's okay. "Hey Mom!" He greeted me with more than a hug, a full frontal attack of joy, like he'd just found something he thought he'd lost, even though it was only an hour after the last bone crunching hug. I'm not complaining. That walk, I could never tell if it was sheepish, because he'd just done something he shouldn't and might get caught; or confident, because he'd just done something he shouldn't and *didn't* get caught. It was a teenager's walk, like *here's my body I don't know what to do with it* mixed with *here's my body, boy, you should see what I can do with it*. The boy has some history.

I don't know why I always refer to "the boy," and "my son," after all, I have two boys, two sons. But somehow this one is always my son, the boy.

That day, he greeted Jesus with that shoulder-bump thing, like testosterone greeting testosterone. Taking the measure of each other, man to man. It was fun to see Jesus like that, and to see the new spirit in my son. He went right up to Jesus, boldly, and said, "Lord, there's something I need to know." There is an earnestness to my son now, an urgency, ever since he came back. Sentence after sentence begins "I need to know, tell me, how is it possible, listen to me, you have to understand." He leans into you, he probes, he pushes. But I give him this, he listens, too. Ever since he's come back it's like he's lost a lifetime and has to make up for it; and he's lived a lifetime and needs to tell you about it. The boy who used to sleep until noon is up before dawn. The boy who never wanted to be around us can't bear to say goodnight. He talks non-stop, not that I press, certainly not for details. I know enough without knowing more than enough, thank you very much. Besides, he had Jesus for that stuff, the bad things, the memories, the nightmares he'd been having. When I saw Jesus take my boy by the elbow and steer him ever so gently away I knew they were headed into territory where mothers are not allowed.

Before walking away, Jesus caught me and said one of those Jesus things that drive you crazy, that make you think so hard your brain hurts until you realize it is true. He says, "Love isn't easy. It's just lovely." It sounds like some wandering holy man jibber-jabber ... but then I got it. The only thing you can count on about love is that it is lovely.

"Look at what I'm doing," Jesus added with a smile, a genuine smile, not a weary smile. "None of this is easy, none of this is obvious, most of it is not given back or understood, or even welcome. But somehow it is always lovely."

I believe him. Trouble had brought him to our house, trouble had stalked him, trouble was in the air. But he didn't seem troubled. The gossip, the rumors, the opposition, the critics; let's face it, the jealousy. All that would have driven me to distraction. It drove him to look deeper, really, really deeper, to find whatever there was that was lovely.

Like my son, that one.

The first time Jesus came here he walked into a hornet's nest, no loveliness apparent. The boy was out of control. I'd like to say he was beside himself because that implies that, here, this is my real boy, and over there is this other boy who shows up from time to time. That would be lovely. But not true. I hate to say this, I'm his mother, but he was mean, selfish, arrogant, cruel, an ugly boy, not lovely.

His father and I asked ourselves *why* a thousand times. We blamed ourselves, the changing times, the neighbors' kids, outside influences, the Romans and how they've corrupted everything and everyone. It's not like it was when we grew up. Kids used to listen to elders, respect tradition. God, country, and family, that was it. I wasn't ready for this one.

The boy was crazy. I know crazy, Jesus knew crazy. One of the troubles that stalked him was what happened with the man called Legion, some crazy fool so full of demons that nothing could control him. What troubled people was that Jesus could control him. The story goes that Jesus and the demons talked together like they knew each other. Then he prayed the demons out of Legion; they went into a herd of pigs and the pigs went scurrying about until they flew off a cliff. The townspeople got mad, believe it or not. I thought that was odd, but when I asked Jesus about it he said, "People are afraid of what they don't understand. They understood demons. They understood Legion as he had been. They didn't understand love."

My son must have looked like another Legion to him. He was shouting, ranting, raving. For weeks he had been demanding – listen to this – his share of the inheritance. Cash. Now. In his hands. As if we were already dead! As if he was a man. As if we can take our sheep, our goats, our fields, our gold pieces, our memories, and, by some tabulation, hand it all to a kid without losing our selves. There was no "please," no "thank you," no plan. At first, we laughed, but not taking him seriously made him angrier. Then we resisted, pressed, asked questions, and it only got worse. I was scared.

When Jesus arrived it should have been overwhelming. A stranger, however holy, shows up in the middle of our family drama, the whole household in an uproar. His disciples were with him, quite a following, but they were respectful, staying off to the side. My other son took charge of them. I could always count on him.

Jesus greeted us that day as if he had always known us. Most days, I like to appear calm but that was beyond me. Instead, we blurted out everything, a torrent of recriminations, despair, and embarrassment. What's he thinking? Who does he think he is? How can he do this to us? What have we done wrong? Jesus may have wondered which of the three of us was crazy, who needed the most help? Of course, he knew. All four of us.

He listened, nodded from time to time, a reassuring touch on the arm, nothing condescending. I wouldn't have thought it possible so quickly, but it seemed as if he fully understood, like he took it all in deep inside. I have heard of the third eye, he had a third ear.

"Excuse me," he said, with a smile, "I'll go see the young man. We have much in common." My other son, observing all this drama, snorted and walked off. "Somebody's got to work around here," he mumbled as he left.

Jesus walked over to the boy, greeted him respect-fully. Leaned in a bit, talking to him, laughing casually. I'm not sure what I expected. Perhaps that Jesus would read him the riot act, shake him up, and draw demons out of him into a flock of crows? Instead, a word, a touch, a smile, another few words. I'd prefer to say that my son punched Jesus in the mouth, or cursed at him so vehe-mently that spittle flew across the front yard. Instead, the boy showed such total disdain – worse, disinterest – like Jesus' thoughts were beneath him. At one point Jesus took something from inside his robe, put it in my son's hand, whispered very earnestly in his ear, put his hand over the boy's hand, and hugged him. Not showy, not forcefully, not tellingly. From a distance it seemed, well, lovely. After weeks of spewed hatred, a hint of lovely. This will sound odd, but it looked like he was putting an im-print, a seal, on our son, right in his palm.

Returning to us Jesus said simply, "Let him go," and taking my husband and me each by an elbow, with him in the middle, we began a healing walk.

He turned the conversation to weather, crops, local politics, aches and pains, done with good humor, easy laughter. Given our family, laughter seemed like a miracle. Strangers are friends you have never met, I've heard, and we were meeting. Jesus' message was clear to all of us – we weren't plotting, we weren't strategizing. We were letting go.

Once back in the main house I had two contradictory responses. First, relief. Someone else had made the decision. It was done. No more fighting. Second, I had a tangle of unsettled questions, mostly "what ifs," with no answers, only worries.

Relief won out. I was too tired. We sat down.

Jesus was no fool. He knew my unsettled questions, my unspoken worries. As we sat he nibbled at the olives, seemed to enjoy the wine. When it was time to leave he gave us advice that sounded strange and felt like a blessing. "Some Legions take longer. And some have to find their own pigs. Let him go. Tell him he's lovely. And fatten up a calf."

After eating, Jesus left. By evening my son was gone.

And then ... the hard work began. It was easy letting him go. It was hell having him gone. We imagined only the worst. Half of our family's history in the hands of a child who hated all we stood for, all we worked for. A boy set loose in the wilds of the world, and I am not exaggerating for effect. I am a mother. Eyes in the back of the head don't stop at the property boundary. So I knew.

At home it was like a funeral every day. The normal pattern is that there's a death, then grieving, then life somehow goes on. For us, it was death and grieving every day. Life didn't go on. We didn't talk. We waited passively for the worst news to be brought to our front door.

It was hardest on our other boy. You see that? We have the boy, and the other boy; my son, and the other son.

How to describe our other son? A good boy. Hardworking, respectful, likeable, treated others the way we'd like to be treated. No, I'm not saying he was perfect, he was real. But his brother sucked all the air out of the room. You can't fight one child all day long and have anything left for the other child. Yes, we took him for granted. His goodness, his dependability, his character, even his love. We assumed it. We had no left over energy to nurture it.

When his brother left, the family diminished; it fell to him to rebuild and restore our family name. We were good for nothing, he had to be good for everything. His father stood each day on the front porch, gazing out at emptiness. I squirreled away inside.

The silence grew louder. The grief grew bitter. A ghost settled in. There was no room for the rest of us. The marriage bed had no marriage. The family dinner had no family. Sabbath brought no rest. Dead, we waited for death.

One afternoon, after countless days and endless nights, I heard a scream, an ungodly uproar, an unimaginable chorus of barnyard animals and household servants consumed by unbelief at something otherworldly unleashed upon our cursed homestead. Running outside, assuming the worst, I saw my husband disappearing down the road, fainter and fainter. He appeared to be jumping.

At that moment, I don't know why, I remembered giving birth to the good son. May I call him that, the good son? It was horrifyingly wonderful, wonderfully painful, painfully beautiful, beautifully bloody, all a miracle. These thoughts of birth filled me up as I waited. Then I heard the shouts, "He's home. He's back. He's here." One even declared, "Young Master has returned! Alive!! Praise God."

"Yes," I thought quickly, "I must praise God. I must fix his room. I must prepare something. I must get his brother." Then I went blank.

The rest of the day was a blur, euphoria and ecstasy underscored by a bigger party than a wedding. Neighbors said he looked like hell. I remember he looked lovely. But he smelled like hell.

My husband? That was a resurrection! Younger than on our wedding day, prouder than when his boys were born, louder than at a neighbor's wedding, he beamed, he soared, he lived again.

My son and I didn't talk that day. We hugged a couple of times, long, gentle embraces. As if we needed to touch each part of the other to know it was really true. The hubbub all around was too much for conversation. A lot of tears, a lot of back slapping, people congratulating me and my husband as if we had done something.

What had we done? We had let him go, as instructed. We left the front gate open. We watched. We waited. We mourned. We prayed. Maybe everybody did their part, my other son most of all. He fattened the calf.

I need his forgiveness, my other son. This feast, this "welcome home from the dead" party, was about an hour old when he walked in. You won't believe it, you shouldn't, but I had forgotten to send for him, to alert him. I should have run to him myself. Before the festivities began, before the neighbors were invited, before the fatted calf was cooked and the wine was poured, I should have been first with this son. I should have said, "Thank you, may God bless you as you have blessed us. Your brother has come home, but we are only a family thanks to you. Come home, this party is for my two sons."

Instead, I forgot him. As always. The second son, born first, always the afterthought. When Jesus was here, the first time, he met briefly with him, a "chin up" talk, and Jesus reminded him that the good we do lives after us, that great is our reward in heaven, that honoring his mother and father was the only Commandment of Moses that came with a promise. Jesus said all the right things and I could tell that boy listened, he took it in. But he deserved more from me and from his father.

Out in the field, he had heard the sounds of the party, one of the laborers filled him in, and he walked slowly to the main house. He stood outside for a while with a cluster of workers who seemed to share his disgust; he poked his head in the door, caught my eye, and left. One boy found, one lost.

The next day was wonderfully still. My boy slept past noon, his father and I sat for the longest time, at peace for the first time in who knows how long. May I say this to you? The wonder of God's grace was all around us. I don't usually talk that way, I don't know such things from study. But sometimes all you are left with is God at work, and this was one of those times. The other boy was absent, but at work, I knew that. It felt like Passover.

The third day was our Easter. The boy was up before anyone, even his brother. He went to the sheds, and then walked the fields, every inch. He saw some day laborers, some long-time workers, greeted them with such exuberance they wondered if it was him.

No one deserved to doubt more than our other boy. And eventually they crossed paths. I know what I feared. And I know a miracle. It was a miracle I saw as I watched them from a distance. When they met, our prodigal son drew close, and touched his brother up high, where the shoulder and arm meet. Then, in a mournful caress, he slid his hand down his brother's arm to the hand, then over to his waist, and bending, down his brother's leg. With no drama he fell to the earth, embracing his brother's feet, kissing one, then the other, and then the ground between them. One lay there. One stood there. That one lifted the other up.

Our religion is built on the Patriarchs. Abraham to Isaac to Jacob. Women, spouses, siblings fade into the background.

Jacob's was the story of two brothers, he and Esau. One cheated his family, one worked hard. One left, one stayed. One fought with God, one served God. One is remembered, one is forgotten. Which is Jacob? Which is Esau? Which one do you remember?

We love our fallen heroes. But it takes more than God to do their saving. When Jacob returned home it was Esau's grace that saved the day. And the family.

It was my other son who saved our day. And our family. He picked his brother up, dusted him off, wiped away the mournful tears, gave him one of those manly, too hard punches to the arm, the one that hurts and feels good at the same time. The one that says "we're good." And they walked home.

Lovely.

He and She

Part I: He

I't was not what he expected, all the contradictory images of hymns and cartoons and the Book of Revelation and Hollywood movies and preachers' exhortations jumbled together. Beulah Land, streets paved with gold, sitting on clouds, playing the harp in the sweet by-and-by in that great gettin' up morning when the saints go marching in. He's still looking for the pearly gates made out of a single pearl.

He remembers a Twilight Zone version of hell. An old couple stuck in a tiny apartment with a psychedelic rock n' roll guitarist. Hell for all three. Maybe so. Maybe this, he thought, is a Twilight Zone heaven. Close, just a little off. Not off in a bad way, just, well, *off*. Odd. Unexpected. It's a little bit of Robin Williams' heaven and Kevin Costner's Field of Dreams. If you can imagine it, it will be; if you build it, they will come.

Maybe he set his sights too low. He never really got Jesus' concept of a celestial condo – "in my father's house are many rooms." The promised grandeur of endless amethyst and sapphire was intriguing, but he took it more allegorically. He didn't strive for Heaven to get mineral deposits. He strove for Heaven to get what he was about to get. She was arriving.

It should be bittersweet, he figured, but he was so focused on the sweet that he didn't taste the bitter. She was arriving. From the moment he got here that thought was never far away. He tried not to obsess over it – he knew the deal. He had a life to live here, she had a life to live there. There were people who had yearned for his arriving, and they made his day every day. Like creation itself, it is good – better than good. And there were people there who yearned for her staying, and they made her day every day. Fair enough, he wouldn't short-circuit that deal on either side. But when the time came, and it was coming, it would put a smile on his face with no apology.

While waiting, he was convivial. There were people floating by on clouds, and playing the harp – some quite well. A few, well – you know what they say, "If you can't say something nice about the dead, don't say anything." It doesn't matter, they seem to enjoy it.

He was not one for the clouds. He was here for the people, God notwithstanding. Now, certainly, there are some folks counting on being in God's presence, 24/7, an eternity with God, non-stop happy, worshipping in some broad sense of the word. And they had that. He neither envied it nor resented it. It reminded him of an ashram he had visited in India, with pious devotees serenely basking in their guru's radiance.

Glad for them. No disrespect intended, not to God or the guru – just making a point. To be with God is wonderful, to have been counted worthy was wonderful, though not entirely expected. But glad to have it. Still, he was here for people, and he got the sense that was okay. A few times he caught God's eye and it was always tender, no judgment, not like, "Gee, what more do you want?!" He felt welcomed and understood.

Still, he probably should have been more sociable. People were exceptionally nice here, that perfect-love-for-everybody as advertised. Everybody he met treated him like their long lost best friend. Folks who had never given him a second thought, coworkers who had never bothered to know his name, neighbors that had not been that neighborly, imperfect church people, imperfect citizens, all those slights given and received now seemed forgotten, replaced by genuine delight. He was glad for this equality, and wanted to measure up. But let's face it, he knew he was more like those people you detest at a party, the ones who pretend to talk with you but are really looking over your shoulder for someone else. Someone more important.

He tried, he really did. Tried to listen, tried to focus, tried to look people in the eye, tried to be fully present. Who was he kidding? There was somebody more important, God forgive him. So his head was always on a swivel, looking over his shoulder, looking past anyone and everything. For her.

He understands others' satisfaction here. He, too, loves the sunsets; the rainbows are spectacular. Heck, paradise is paradise, that ought to be good enough. Plus, "until death do us part" puts an expiration date right there on the marriage vows. Right? It's over. Done. Move on. Maybe she did move on. Maybe everyone here moved on, happy on their cloud, happy with God, happy with everybody. Content. Content is a good word. Happy is a good word. More than happy, ecstatic. Fulfilled. Whole. God bless 'em.

He is definitely not whole. Not fulfilled. Not content.

But, to be fair, he's not grumpy. He's not disappointed or complaining. Heaven is truly heavenly. The lion and the lamb really do lie down together. All the people we are supposed to help on earth in order to get to heaven – the hungry, the thirsty, the naked, the imprisoned – well, they're not hungry, thirsty, naked or imprisoned. The sick aren't sick anymore. The sinners are forgiven. The miserable have lost their misery, the lost are found, the tears are wiped away. The dead aren't dead anymore. There is a balm in Gilead. He always loved that hymn, and it turns out to be true.

Not that he talks about that with anyone, except in his prayers, but he would want everyone to know heaven is wonderful. He never took that Book of Revelation stuff too seriously, at least not the descriptions of horrors and wonders. The wonder is heaven – the horror is to miss it.

Somehow, he didn't miss it; he'd made the cut. He had always told people when he was alive – earthly alive, that is – that if he got into heaven, it would be on her coattails, not by his own doing. That wasn't meant as self-deprecation. He was always honest to a fault, even his own faults. He knew where he stood, and when it came to heaven he should have stood on the outside looking in. Instead, he's on the inside – looking and waiting.

Some people question him. Not judgmentally; there's none of that around here. But they are surprised to see him in any way unsettled, and maybe they find that unsettling, which only unsettled him more. So to settle everyone down he tried to explain it logically, which here meant Biblically. He was not one for Bible-thumping, but he liked the Bible, respected it, found comfort in it.

One afternoon, under some gentle questioning, he reminded these neighbors that in the original Paradise Adam was unsettled for a bit. Isn't that so? Even God noticed. All creation was pairing up, finding their own complement; only Adam remained alone – isn't that so? Metaphorically, if you will, or literally if you so choose, God gave Eve to Adam from Adam's own rib. *I'm just waiting to get my rib back,* he told them, with a smile that surprised them enough to end their questions and their concern. That settled, he felt invigorated, which triggered more memories. He had had a favorite city, he told them, a place that life had taken him to only once, on his own. Everything he loved had been right at his fingertips. Music, art, history, absinthe, inspiration. It *should* have been his own personal heaven on earth – but it wasn't heaven without her there. People nodded sympathetically at a story they knew well.

So, he waited. With patience. Humor, candor and patience – that was his method. He hoped, sincerely, that she loved her life. The kids, the grandkids, they needed her, they doted on her. To lose her would be devastating, irreplaceable. He wouldn't wish that sorrow on anyone. His waiting wasn't tinged with resentment or exasperation. It was just waiting. Things go better with Coke? No, not here. Things go better with her, that's all. Even heaven. And it was about to get better.

Part II: She

That night, she laid herself down to sleep, as the words of the children's prayer drifted through her mind, called up from distant memory, frightening and yet magically comforting:

> *Now I lay me down to sleep*
> *I pray the Lord my soul to keep.*
> *If I should die before I wake*
> *I pray the Lord my soul to take.*

She knew that the time for her soul-keeping was up, and that the time for her soul-taking had arrived. She'd seen enough of death to know it. Grandparents, one by one. Parents, one by one. Friends, one by one. Him, her one and only. The children's poem was true; so was the Bible: *a time to live, a time to die.* When you are living, it is never the right time to die. But after, maybe it is all good. She believed that.

When the time had come for his soul to be taken, she had done her best to keep her soul occupied. No, not occupied – that sounds like resignation, like she just put in her time from then until now. That wasn't her way. She had the gift to be fully present wherever she was, with whomever. She refused to live out her days with regrets, or living in the clouds. When the clouds came for her, fine. Until then, let the sun shine.

Other people had their say, friends mostly. Well-intentioned. The busyness of the days just after his death was a Godsend. Phone calls, funeral planning, people dropping in, the best casseroles. Her family, of course, their family.

She enjoyed the funeral planning, partly because she knew it would annoy him so, as she told everybody. He'd said, I don't want a fuss. I lived a normal life. Didn't do much worth mentioning. Everything is in order. Gather the kids, you can have the Reverend say a prayer. Then take the family to that restaurant we always went to, on us. Tell that grandson to have the steak. Of course, she assured him. Of course. No fuss. Well, maybe a little fuss.

The Reverend asked if he could come by, but she preferred to meet in the church. There they put together a nice, old-fashioned, simple, dignified funeral service. A good hymn, not a maudlin one. The children who wanted to speak would speak, the ones who were hesitant to speak would speak. The grandchildren would speak on her behalf, and do some readings. The Reverend would make sense of it all: life, work, family, faith, and Psalm 1. A good service for a good man. A good bye. Until.

After the funeral she thought she would surely sleep for a week. Instead, the next day she found herself up at six, making a full breakfast. It dawned on her too slowly that she had cooked for two, set the table for two.

People were kind, in their way. First were the friends who wanted to keep her busy, as if she were a three-year-old who needed babysitting. It was annoying, but she didn't let on.

Second were the matchmakers. They all kept a list of recent widowers on file. The match of choice she called Mr. Greenjeans. He'll fix that screen door that's been broken forever, she was promised. Maybe I *like* that screen door broken, she said, not quite out loud. After all, it was her he who had broken it and left it broken. She didn't need another he who would fix it. She was the fixer. They had made a good match, the breaker and the fixer. She laughed inside.

She was not irritated by all her advisers and matchmakers, however insistent or even crude. It all came from a good place; it just wasn't her place. She wasn't looking to be fixed, matched, mated, occupied or otherwise distracted. Not that she was a recluse, or depressed. She was not grief-stricken, or heartbroken; her heart was quite fine, thank you very much; and her grief was proper, well-earned and private. She was neither secretly relieved nor eerily peaceful. And she was definitely not in denial. She knew death well. Its look, its smell, its touch. Its absence. She could do stiff upper lip, she could do tears, she could sigh, smile, reminisce, miss, and move on (wink, wink). When required.

Truth was, she had a job that kept her busy. And there was still time for lunch with friends, trips to the library, gardening, helping at church, visiting shut-ins.

Her job, a job she'd assigned herself, was creating his legacy. He always said if he got into heaven it would only be on her coattails, which always got a laugh, even from her, but it did bother her. She knew he meant it, and she knew he was wrong, and she was going to train up two generations that got it right, and after that was done then she would pray the Lord her soul to take.

So, she worked on his legacy. Stories told, lessons learned, memories kept, all very much in the present tense. She remembered that her Jewish neighbors had invited them to Passover a few times. Lots of wine, plenty of food, the Bible treated like a living book. And always, one seat left unoccupied, just in case Elijah was to come to dinner. Like the Motel 6 ad, "We've kept the porch light on." At her home – their home – she kept the porch light on. And one chair empty.

Legacy is a big word, she realized. She wasn't a Rockefeller leaving a thousand acres of pristine forest to create a nature reserve. She wasn't giving ten million dollars to a university to endow a chair in Eastern European dark novels. But she would leave her family with a living testimonial to him, and, she guessed, to them – him and her. Something worth remembering, but it required a soft touch, almost casual. Not a four star TED Talk on "The Life and Times of Him." Legacy, not monument.

She set about creating remembrances, complicated by remembrances. It was a paradox. The children always talked about remembrances from when they were little. And the grandchildren only remembered him as old. Not doddering and drooling old, but gray and rumpled and sitting still old. That wasn't right for someone who hated sitting and was never rumpled until the bitter end overcame him. Her thousand acres, $10 million legacy gift was to clear away the nostalgia and the bitter end. Let him breathe again. She would reintroduce her Elijah to the family. The other poor Elijah, all he is remembered for is being swept away to heaven. Which set her to humming:

Swing low, swing chariot,
comin' for to carry me home.
I looked over Jordan and what did I see?
A band of angels comin' after me.
Comin' for to carry me home.

Maybe at the time that is how it appears. But until that time there is a lot more left to be said, and she would say it. Gently and firmly. She laughed, remembering that the old Biblical Elijah hadn't wanted a fuss, either.

In turns subtle and sweet, never pointed, she would tell her Elijah's story, the living that went on between childhood memories and the "Rumpled-stiltskin" years, as he would call himself. She smiled. The approach? Not larger than life, not heroic; he didn't need to be bronzed. Maybe painted, as it were. They both had liked art. Neither one could draw a straight line. But they spent years looking at everyone else's lines: straight, squiggly, swirling. Yes, she decided, that was it: she was, at last, painting. Maybe he is chuckling, but in an encouraging way. He always encouraged, even when correcting.

They loved impressionism. Not pointillism: "too pointed," he critiqued, dead serious. And not Hopper's realism: "too real," he remarked, just as seriously. Impressionism, so you can feel it. That's what she wanted. That's what she missed. Feeling him.

Her plan was to return the feeling to the memories. This was for the children and grandchildren. His legacy, his and hers. Theirs too, one day, but she would leave it to them to make it theirs. Her job was his legacy.

Amazingly, they embraced it. At first it seemed they were humoring her. But you can't fake mist in your eyes, even while rolling them. All in all, it required a delicate balance. She would tell stories of him doing just the right thing at just the right time, or saying what needed to be said before it was obvious. For someone of his generation it bothered him how often injustices of the ugliest kind kept appearing and reappearing. We're going backwards, was his exasperated refrain, I've wasted my life. Then he'd plot revenge, to right some wrong without crossing over to the wrong, though some wrongs tempted him.

The fisticuffs of his youth could have been better used as an adult, he was quite sure. Instead, he fought with words as cudgels. The words could come in a torrent. The kids would brag to their friends that they were never punished, not even given a curfew. But he could talk at a length that broke the Geneva Conventions.

And then there were the letters he wrote: to the children, to friends, to anyone he thought needed to hear from him. An alignment of nouns, verbs and adjectives that devoured whole trees to make a single point. Folks said that the groups he joined ran smoothly because everyone wanted to avoid his scribbled ten-page letters of suggestions.

But he saved his best words, his most complex, run-on sentences with no punctuation, for his thoughts about injustice. It was his conviction, with some evidence, that whole armies of people across the globe got up each morning with no other purpose than to make someone's life miserable. And it was his purpose in life to get up each morning and point out that absurdity. His plethora of words, usually handwritten, often hand-delivered, turned up in the mailboxes of countless town officials, school board committees, and editors of newspapers local and international. When published, his letters elicited the highest volume of response, and the most incendiary. That was a good day. The mentors of his life had been word warriors; he had learned from the best, he said proudly.

He believed in the power of the written word, the spoken word, the shouted word, the ironic word, and above all, the repeated word.

He would have laughed at this idea of legacy. The only possession he laid claim to was his books, and possessed is the right word, she thought. His books were everywhere, organized by a system so secret he took it with him. She tried the obvious. Topic? Author? No. Size, color, font? No. But heaven forbid one got moved by the occasional housecleaning. "Where is that book by what's his name?" he would bellow across the house. "What's the title?" "I don't remember." "What does it look like?" "That doesn't matter, it was right there, and now it's not there." Another priceless treasure lost to the ages, all part of a plot, he was sure, to rid the world of good words.

His life unfurled from page to page. All the ideas and issues of his universe were in those books, enhanced by his own margin notes, highlights and dog-ears. Ready to be passed on. Don't you dare leave those to me, one of their children protested, unless they're catalogued and boxed. Afterwards, another child came over to help catalogue, but couldn't bring herself to box. Together, the two of them would open a book, note the words, jot them down, return it to the proper place. And wipe their eyes.

She decided that they, all of them, should know about Joan of Arc. That was strange enough to catch their attention. Yes, Joan of Arc. He'd loved Joan of Arc, the Ingrid Bergman version. Then came the day they'd made a day trip from Paris to Rouen. He'd wandered the town wide-eyed, following Joan's last footsteps, overwhelmed by her courage, her youthful hope, her terror. They'd gone to the tower where she was imprisoned, to the place where she was burned at the stake, to the riverside where her ashes were discarded. He had wept.

The family listened nicely, but puzzled. They'd known his affection for obscure authors, for social justice heroes; they knew his Ted Williams obsession, and Don Quixote. But Joan of Arc?

Voices, she explained, immediately upping the worry level. Joan heard voices and went up against implacable forces; that's how he had explained his love for her story. It was both a rhyme and a partnership, voices against forces. In the retelling, she was bemused that they still didn't get it.

Did he hear voices, they asked, hesitantly? She knew they were open to either answer. Each led down an interesting path, and they all loved interesting paths. Robert Frost for all.

She never pressed him on voices. It was part of his interior life, and she respected that. He shared everything but secrets, she told him, only a little annoyed. And despite his lofty heroes, stories of him doing the right thing were followed, in his telling and hers, by stories of doing the wrong thing. He certainly did not need to be humanized for them, that's for sure: there were enough stories of bad turns, bad timing, mixed signals, awful ideas. He always arrived too early, left too soon, forgot something, spilled something or missed something. He was the object of his own humor. Her job, their legacy, was to rearrange the moments of organic despair with a lifetime of righteous indignation, tinged with laughter and hope. Melancholy joy with a purpose.

Thank goodness this was only for family. For anyone else it would be such a bore, a paean to self-flagellation, to coin his phrase. It took many forms. Stories, phrases, failures, laughter, imagination, music. In her telling, always with a point, gently. All to say he had been here. It mattered. You should matter.

As time went on, she seemed smaller. Not diminished but, yes, actually smaller. With each occasion, each telling, it was as though she was giving part of herself. She felt it. She was aware. She remembered going to estate sales – oh, how he hated that. If you've got something left at the end then you've got too much, he grumbled, and not under his breath. Nevertheless, he always bought a book. Looks like a 4th edition in exemplary state, he would say too loud to everyone in particular. Like an estate sale, she was being emptied piece by piece, something precious going out the door whenever the family left. It was a good feeling.

As she grew smaller, she felt stronger, as if unburdened made her lighter on her feet. In church, she took to sitting down front. Not the back-corner pew he had always guided them to. Now she focused clearer. The scriptures sounded more personal, the sermon more real, the cross more important. Later, at coffee hour, she always thanked whomever gave the altar flowers.

The first Sunday that she gave the flowers in memory of him, she came to church much earlier than usual, before the ushers, and she sat quite still in her near-front pew. No one saw her tears. Her family arrived during the opening hymn, filling almost three pews. She was proud. At sermon time the Reverend was about to read the scripture, but, without looking up, mentioned that the verses had been often suggested to him by a member. Hear the word of the Lord, he said, from the prophet Micah, Chapter Six, Verse Eight. You know, O man, what is good; and what does the Lord require of you but to do justice, love mercy, and walk humbly with your God? She was surprised that he used the old version – *you know, O man*. The Reverend nodded at her, imperceptibly.

At the coffee hour, one of the ladies brought her the flowers to take to the grave, but she asked for them to stay on the altar for the day – if that was alright. It seemed to please them both. The family thought to go out to dinner, but she preferred their own dining room table. He had always loved Thanksgiving. And even though it was early autumn, when they walked through the door the table looked like Thanksgiving. Whatever she always made was there, what they always liked was there, whatever he always required was there. Plates were passed, wine poured, conversation flowed, time stood still. Stories were told seamlessly as if picked up from the exact point where they left off previously, regardless of who left off, or when. They included her fully, always looking directly at her as talk shifted gears, occasionally waiting for her thought. Today she mostly listened, as though she was not required. From time to time, a grandchild would come over for a hug, a caress, a question. Whenever one of the kids got up for something, they always walked near her, touched her shoulder; she would touch their hand with her cheek.

When it seemed the time for leaving, they insisted on cleaning up. She wouldn't hear of it, and they wouldn't hear of not hearing of it, so it all got done. They poured her one more wine, let her oversee their efforts, returning everything to its proper place – from the special dishes to platters that had been wedding gifts. With lingering hugs and wet kisses, they made their departures. She closed the screen door only, walked to the sitting room, chose to sit in his reading chair. She would lay herself down to sleep just for the twinkling of an eye, as she always promised him.

Part III: He

On the other side, life was stirring, sensations he remembered from New England mornings, a crispness that meant apples and harvest. It would be a good day.

This place is a miracle of hustling bustle, he realized, the constant surprise of arrivals and reunions all achieved with unusual grace and calm. For a moment it felt like their favorite restaurant in Florence, on what they always called their side of the river. A place so tiny, with customers on the inside and hopefuls on the outside, a frenzied artistry done with aplomb. Those were her words. He was at the corner table, one chair empty, two glasses poured, the candle lit. As the screen door opened.

A Church for Christopher Hitchens

The hometown paper of a little Southern town says it's Maundy Thursday, the start of Holy Week. Not counting Palm Sunday. Who counts Palm Sunday? It's the serious stuff that matters, right? Last Supper, Gethsemane, Judas and his 30 pieces of silver, Peter's denial till the cock crows, Mel Gibson's endless Passion from whips to cross, a dead Jesus, a silent Saturday. Easter.

On the Religion page, little two by one inch ads for Holy Week services at local churches hit me hard, someplace unexpected, someplace I didn't know I had, someplace I had forgotten: childhood church in an age of belief, in a neighborhood of belief. Even the bad guys believed. Or went to church, it was the same thing. We all smoked, we all went to Mass, we all played ball, we all hung on corners, we were all James Dean. We could pout, slouch, snicker, and cross ourselves all at the same time. Pink Spaldeen, zip gun and confessional, and we were ready for daily life. Forgiven just enough to keep rolling.

When not James Dean-ing the neighborhood, doo-wopping the street corners, or living the Blackboard Jungle, we were playing pick-up, which had nothing to do with girls. Stickball sewer to sewer, sandlot baseball, the asphalt games of slap ball and basketball, they all began with pick-up, choosing sides from whoever could get there.

Whoever could get there was determined by the rhythms of religion played out on us, our siblings, the next door neighbor's kids, and a whole universe called the relatives. There were eight million stories in the Naked City and we were related to half of them, all bound to religion. Baptism. First Communion. Confirmation. Released Time. Confession. Saturday Mass. Sunday School. The mothers on the block had more Holy Days of Obligation than the Pope. And more authority.

In between religion we squeezed in what we could. Even what we could smelled of religion. You know what the C stands for in CYO? YMCA? Meant something in those days. Dances, friends, teams. We learned our moves not far from any church. Any church was not far from us.

All this comes flooding my little brain looking at tiny ads for Holy Week services. They stir convoluted memories, and contradictory thoughts. Stern sermons, hypocritical parishioners, hard doctrines, mixed in with church basements, pot luck suppers, church ladies, fast friendships, an air of mystery, a hint of magic, a touch of the divine.

Lost in midlife, I am far from the neighborhood of my youthful innocence, transgressions, and belief. Now I am way down south in more ways than one, and about to lose it all.

With a knot in my stomach, tied up with nostalgia, I put the paper down, pick it up, turn the page, go back to the page, rip out the ad, put it in my tweed jacket inside pocket where important pieces of paper go to be forgotten.

Instead, I remember.

As a kid we had a Lenten Dime Folder that stood prominently at the center of the kitchen table. At dinner each kid stuck in a dime for some sacrifice they made that day. Didn't buy a comic book. Didn't smoke. Didn't swear. Forty slots for forty dime sacrifices. I was about to give up a night of binge TV watching. Maybe that was worth a dime.

Late that afternoon I drive to the next town, splurge on some fast food pizza, then drive around looking for an unlikely Lutheran church in a world full of Southern Baptists.

I find it, as the Tiffany-inspired bumper stickers boasted in the 70s, a guilt encrusted taunt at those who lost it. God, my mind is a mess, maybe this isn't such a good idea. But, there it is, so I get out of the car to continue my unlikely pilgrimage.

Outside there are no vast hordes, thus decreasing my chances of anonymity; and nobody I knew, thus decreasing my chances of embarrassment. What if I've forgotten when to kneel, how to cross, what to say? Strange to be entering into something so familiar feeling like a stranger. Stranger, still, to walk into the House of God minus God. One of us has been away.

I am about to end Lent by taking up what I had given up. I hope somebody was enjoying the irony in all this.

It is a nondescript church but when I push through the simple, dark wood doors into the sanctuary, trumpets blare like medieval heraldry, the organ builds to a crescendo, and a thousand people turn around to stare at me. Whether they are welcoming or judging is hard to say. The austere priest up on the altar, dressed in his best Jesus-is-almost-dead vestments, stands between me and the altar like a stop sign.

I stop.

Of course, this is all in my head. Guilt isn't good for much, but it stokes the imagination. Ever read Dante's *Divine Comedy*? Believe me, every guilty soul gets their just desserts in deliciously evil ways. That's the comedy part, I guess. God is no slacker when it comes to getting even. He's liking tonight.

So I am in the church, my guard is up, my conscience is working overtime, I'm hallucinating, they are about to do the Prayer of Confession and I'm ready to confess to anything to get out of there. I could duck out but there's only about twenty people in the church. Walking out would add insult to injury, extending my confession deficit.

I reach for the nearest pew, slide in, sit down, open the bulletin, find the prayer book, pretend to know the routine.

Right away there's a hand on my knee. A woman's hand, with a wedding ring on it. And she's leaning in, softly squeezing my knee. Her hand is trembling, my knee is trembling, I'm trembling. Maybe if I look straight ahead, or turn the page. Maybe it's time to stand; please, God, let's read the Gospel or do one of those Doxologies, anything that puts us on our feet. You need a reader,

Father? Call me up. Glass of water, extra usher, I'm your man. Just get me out of here.

Her hand on my knee grows insistent, more intimate. I'm a goner. This is going to end badly. I'm going to be tarred and feathered in a Heat of the Night southern town and tomorrow's paper will headline "Yankee Carpetbagger Assaults Homecoming Queen in Church."

How long is this Prayer of Confession? Can I get an Amen? Time for the damn offering or sing a hymn. Don't you do Holy Communion in this stupid church? I thought that's what Maundy Thursday is for. I know that much. Doesn't everybody go down front? That's right. We stand up, go down the aisle, kneel at the railing, come on, let's do it.

Her lips are at my ear, whispering, her hand still on my knee, maybe higher.

"You're sitting in my husband's seat."

I turn to look at her. Yes, a true flower of southern beauty, 85 years old or more.

"For almost 60 years we have sat together in this very pew, side by side, I in this very same space, he where you are now."

No reproach in her words, she is too genteel to offer reproach to a stranger for an unintended faux pas, however rude.

Swedes blush red, and I am in full blush, trying to extricate myself without causing a scene. I put my bulletin in the prayer book, nod an embarrassed apology, lean forward to start my standing-up exit. Good excuse to leave.

"No, no," she says with sweet insistence, the one hand firmer still on my knee, surprisingly strong, keeping me in my seat.

"He died. You stay. He would be so happy to see you here."

Thirteen words spoken with such love, such sorrow, such faith, accompanied by her extraordinary determination, keep me wedded to that sacred space.

Holy Communion.

Still Swedish, still blushing, still guilty, for the next hour I belong to her. She holds my hand, guides me through the prayer book in the most subtle way, gently nudging me up and pulling me down as liturgy requires. At offering time she opens her purse with one hand, not letting go of me with the other, and produces a five dollar bill for me to give. "That's what we always did," she explains, but I already know. When I put the money in the offering plate, the usher bows ever so slightly, respecting far more than the five dollars.

"Praise God from whom all blessings flow," we sing. "Amen to that," I think.

I sit down. Start reflecting. People talk about time standing still at certain epiphany points in life. Everything happening in slow motion. Each word leaves a mark. We say that after. During, it just is. Thus we sit, side by side, hand in hand. Hours, weeks, years, two lifetimes merged in a single pew. One lived a tad higher than the other; one with more sorrow known, the other with more sorrow caused; one remembering, the other hoping to forget.

Sermons were never my favorite part of church. Someone who knew nothing about me laying into me about something they knew nothing about. Op-ed pieces wrapped in religion. Lectures, threats. Irrelevance. Boredom. Now those are cardinal sins.

Against those expectations my austere priest takes the pulpit. Maundy Thursday and Good Friday provide a tandem of despair. Seriously, what goes on those two days? An ode to gore, pornographic violence, human nature reverting to savagery. You've got the first Judas goat. You've got Jesus' friends lying and fleeing. You've got the birth of anti-Semitism. Pilate washing his hands of it all. Enough torture to end the debate on torture. Good fodder for a hell-fire and brimstone sermon.

Not tonight. Sentence by sentence he crafts a caress.

"What did Jesus see?" the priest asks. Lutherans have priests, right? In my neighborhood all clergy were priests, except the nuns. We even called the Rabbi "Father."

"What did Jesus see?" was the question of the night. When he looked in Judas' eyes before Judas took off to collect his fee? When he looked at Peter bragging to the rafters that he'd never deny him? When he looked at the disciples sound asleep while he sweat blood in Gethsemane? When he looked at the soldier about to raise the hammer to pound the nail into his wrist? When he looked at the guy next to him being crucified, who seemed to believe a little, and the other who had no hope at all? When he looked at his mother one last time?

What did he see that enabled him to say, with almost his last breath, 'Forgive them, for they know not what they do'?"

In case any of us are entirely dense, the priest quite nicely invites each of us to let Jesus look into our eyes and let him see what he can see that would let him let us off the hook.

Let Jesus look into my eyes to see what he can see. No, thank you. Jesus let the worst of the worst off the hook because they "know not what they do." What about those who know damn well what we do? Or is that the point? That I have no idea what I'm doing, even if I think I do?

At this point I grit my teeth hard, she squeezes my hand.

The hymn before Communion is a tear jerker, and neither of us needs the help. Whatever she's thinking and whatever I'm thinking are worlds apart, separated by three inches on a wooden pew. Maybe there are no worlds apart.

We stand to sing, holding hands, cradling the spine of the hymnbook. "That's what we always did," she explains, but I already knew. We sing an old hymn full of irony, but no more so than the two of us in harmony.

In the cross of Christ I glory,
towering o'er the wrecks of time;
all the light of sacred story
gathers round its head sublime.
When the woes of life o'er take me,
hopes deceive, and fears annoy,
never shall the cross for-sake me;
lo! it glows with peace and joy.
When the sun of bliss is beaming
light and love upon my way,

from the cross the radiance streaming
adds new luster to the day.
Bane and blessing, pain and pleasure,
by the cross are sanctified;
peace is there, that knows no measure,
joys that through all time abide.

Then, Holy Communion. Or maybe we just had it. Either way, it sneaks up on me, even though it was in the bulletin and on the altar. But it isn't for me.

In my world, Communion was tricky business. Who got it, who didn't, why they didn't, what to do, what it is. Some don't deserve it, some don't believe it. It's funny. Communion means coming together. Holy means setting apart. How am I supposed to figure that out?

The way of least resistance is to stay put, don't go up front. It would look humble and people like that. Save everybody the embarrassment of turning me away at the altar rail.

The priest does his thing, graceful in more ways than one. He has a way of telling the story without talking down to us. I get the Holy part, and the Communion part, but it still is not for me.

As people start to go forward I stand up to let her pass. She steps into the aisle, then takes my arm firmly and won't let go. Drawing very close she explains, "This is how we always did it." But I already know that.

Everyone else is single file down the aisle; we are side by side, hand in hand. When our turn comes I start to use my free hand to *no, thank you* the priest — but she squeezes the other hand with strength I never guessed was there. It hurts enough to wake something up in me.

The priest looks at me like Jesus in his sermon. What is he seeing? Judas? Peter? The Good Thief? The not so good thief?

I dare not move. He puts the bread in my mouth, brings the chalice to my lips, nods to me to drink.

As sacrilegious teens we laughed at the cannibalism, with the smirky joke, "eat my flesh, drink my blood," hoping to sound blasphemous. We mocked churches that used grape juice instead of wine. We puzzled over Transubstantiation. So, what is it tonight? God just fed me. Make of that what you will. God. Fed. Me. And I am the substance being changed. I don't know how, or why. I have a pretty good idea about who. She squeezes my hand again, and leads us back to our pew. Just as she always did.

As the service ends, the church gets darker and the priest stands at the front with a tall candle. Briefly, he reminds us of what is still to come. The awfulness of Good Friday. The silence of Saturday. The miracle of Sunday. Then he says:

> Go forth into the world to serve God with gladness; be of good courage; hold fast to that which is good; render to no one evil for evil; strengthen the fainthearted; support the weak; help the afflicted; honor all people; love and serve God, rejoicing in the power of the Holy Spirit. The grace of Jesus Christ, the love of God, and the communion of the Holy Spirit be with you all. Amen.

Suddenly, it is done. Over. People get up to leave. She leans over and kisses me. "This is what we always did," she explains, and I squeeze her hand. I figure he did that.

The priest stands at the door, saying good night to folks. When he shakes my hand he says, "Feed my sheep," twice like that, quietly, urgently, personally. He probably said that to all the people, but I am the last one out, she still holding my hand. "Feed my sheep," he says, a third time, looking me in the eye.

She insists on walking me to my car, me being the stranger and all, old fashioned hospitality.

By the car, as we part, I ask her, "What does Maundy mean?"

"It's Latin," she explains. "Command."

I don't get it.

"Love," she says, blushing. "At the Last Supper Jesus gives a new command. Love."

But I already know that.

Papa

"Papa!"

She bounds into the room, full of eighteen-year-old life. His roommate and the nurse's aide can feel it. It feels good. Papa reflects the sunshine that just entered the room.

"How nice of you to come!" he exults with absolute sincerity, even if he was not quite sure of their relation. He knew enough that it was special. And she was here. That's all it took to make a good day.

She introduced herself to the others, covering nicely for his uncertainty. "I'm his great granddaughter, we used to live in India, but now I'm in college. We have the Jewish Holy Day off, so I came up for the day."

He liked that, she said Holy Day, not holiday, like it was still important. He always liked the Holy Days, theirs, his, they felt like ours. He liked the nursing home. Every day looked like a Holy Day. The men with long white beards, dressed in long black coats with big fur hats, the visitors, and the people, too, even his roommate. Maybe he will grow a beard. Yesterday a nice person asked if he was Jewish. Yes, mostly, he had said, we are all Jewish, or none of us are, which seemed to puzzle the nice lady.

"Rabbi Benjamin, he was a good friend," Papa told his great granddaughter. He didn't often strike up a conversation anymore. People thought he didn't hear, or couldn't remember, a gentle Alzheimer's. Maybe he just retired from words, he had used so many in his life. Seventy years of preaching. Five thousand meetings. Not enough years of marriage. Short stories written for the Saturday Evening Post. Never published, but the words still counted. He loved words. His love of Latin was rooted in words. Know Latin, know words. That was his SAT prep advice for every teenager. His great granddaughter remembered.

"Rabbi Ben and I, we loved Queens. We thought everything ran through his synagogue and my church. Or it should. Theology, politics, scripture. Playing handball in Victory Park, we would resolve all the issues of the universe. Then he would defeat me, 50% of the time."

Papa let that last paradox hang in the air. She smiled at his smile, surprised he was so talkative. Family had warned her not to expect much. But she had expectations anyway.

"Did you go to church?" he asked her. It wasn't Sunday. Did he mean today, or ever? Did he remember her blended background? "Hare Christian," her mother called her. A poster in her room proclaimed, "My God is too big for one religion." She stole it from her mother.

"I go to church sometimes, but not today," she answered, a bit puzzled.

"That's good, it's not Sunday, you know." Was that a "gotcha" moment?

"Papa, church is so important to you, it has been your whole life. And God, and the Bible, and Jesus. I respect that, very much. I'm taking World Religions in college, and at my school people are everything. Wiccans and Pagans, and so many kinds of Christians, most I've never heard of. Clubs for Muslims, Hindus. Yoga all the time. They don't even know it's part of religion, Papa! Then there are the atheists, agnostics, people angry at some religion or all religion. Most of my college friends make fun of religion, or grew up without any, so I can't really talk with them. But you've given your whole life to it. Maybe you would help me?"

He watched her so intently, and heard the appeal in her voice, and in her eyes. She meant it. My whole life, she had said, repeating it in his mind. Isn't that something! She's right, of course, not quite certain how she knows that.

And, she wants my help. Nobody has needed my help in a long time, the thought forming in his head but making it public on his face before responding, "All that at your college? That is wonderful, so many thinking about the same thing but in different ways. I should go there."

She imagined wheeling him out of the nursing home, squeezing him into her Uber, driving to college, bringing him to classes for a day.

"Papa. Maybe you can help me with my course. I have to do a Faith Timeline about my religious life. Maybe you can show me. Tell what you knew, and when you knew it, and how it changed to where you are now with your beliefs. Would you do that with me?"

He paused a long time. Looked around, smiled at someone out in the hallway, took a sip of tea. She had remembered to bring him one tea and a slice of chocolate mousse cake from nearby. He opened the container, chuckled, and very slowly took a mouthful.

"When I was little we were always in church. That never changed. From then till now, church. That deserves another piece of cake," which he took with obvious delight.

"Do you like to look up?" It was asked with a smile. Everything comes with a smile. If Papa ever scowled it was in days gone by. "I was always a runner. I ran to the ballfield. I ran to school, ran to church, ran for fun, I never got tired. Because, I always looked up."

The point seemed obvious to him but his hearers wanted more. It's nice when people want more.

"I don't know, Papa, I never liked running much. I never saw the point."

He laughed. "Most people, when they run, they look down, pounding the pavement, like that is the purpose. Pounding is tiring. I always looked up."

There was a pause. The great granddaughter knew, somehow, that there was something holy at work here, here in this moment when blood was meeting blood.

He spoke again. "So you've come from India! Isn't that something!" He sounded as enthusiastic as if she had come all that way just to see him. Perhaps so. She didn't correct him.

"Yes, Papa."

"I was there, once. I don't remember why. But it was most impressive. What did you do there?"

She did not want to sound condescending, and she was afraid of embarrassing him with an answer that might remind him of what he should know.

"I'm glad you liked India, Papa. People there still remember you and when I was living there I would always tell about you. For my school I wrote a report about you, and on the cover I put a photograph of you visiting an Indian Church where they honored you with garlands and a shawl. You are almost buried under the flowers!"

"Oh, no, let's not talk of burial yet, I have miles to go before I sleep. Robert Frost, you know."

"Yes, Papa, *Stopping by Woods on a Snowy Evening.*"

"Well," he said with obvious satisfaction, "you study poetry in your school in India, that is a good school."

Ok, she thought, he knows more than he lets on, or it comes in bits and pieces, or one idea lets loose another. What an interesting man.

"What do you think is really important, Papa?"

He looks at her with another great smile, the kind of smile they call beatific. It really is. But he doesn't say anything, just yet. Instead, he's on a journey in his mind. People think his mind wanders. No, it wonders, he says to himself. Wonders, not wanders, I like that. He chuckles, out loud, and has another forkful of cake.

He enjoys the journey in his mind. No one speaks over him. Or ignores him. Of course, she wouldn't. Still, he wonders, should I tell her about marching with Martin Luther King, Jr., in Alabama? We turned the corner toward the state capitol, all I could see were Confederate flags, and people so angry they had spittle drooling down their lips, hanging from their chin.

She's watching him closely, as he seemed to shudder. It wasn't very attractive, he remembers, or hygienic. But the walk was. Attractive, and hygienic. Good for the soul, at least mine. We have our own sheets in the closet, I was told once. I won't mention that.

He looked at his great granddaughter and felt her intensity. He liked that in a person. It showed commitment. Should I tell her about our last child, born a blue baby, we didn't know if she would survive? She did, you know, she became a fine person, you would like her. Maybe you're related, you look like her. Hmmm.

What is important, she asked me? I like that question, it is a wise question. She must be a good student. And to think, she is here, with me. Yes, she came all this way to see me.

He looks at her closely. "I think you are important," he says out loud rather forcefully.

He said far more with those words, full of affirmation and pride and gratitude, and she heard them all fully. Being here together is important, they both say silently at the same time. She had been hoping for something more profound. Instead, she got something more profound. It was her turn to smile.

"Do you read the Bible?" he asks.

He doesn't say it like a test, he never does, she had always heard that about him. That he never asked anything just to ask, or to embarrass, or to test. He asked because he wanted to know. To probe. Every question created an answer, the start of a conversation, an opportunity to learn. What better way to spend time?

"I have a Bible, Papa. Sometimes I open it up randomly, but I don't really know it. I think there must be some secret to it. Now I am studying religions, but maybe I should take a course next semester about the Bible. And whenever I have questions you can teach me."

"There are stories there that will teach you what is important" he said with surprising power.

Aha. He returned to a topic from before, she realized. There is definitely more going on inside than he chooses to bring out. She surprised herself, thinking that's sort of cool, an interior world where he is fully alive. They will show you something important, he just told her. She wondered if he was going to call her Grasshopper, like that old Kung Fu TV show. She felt she was on the verge of something.

He felt he was on the verge of something. Her earnestness was like a wood stove warming every room inside the mansion of his mind. He remembered an old story, maybe a folk tale, which said the best way to remember was to build a memory palace, and fill it room by room with all that is precious. It works. Room by room this young lady is taking me on a tour. I hope we can stop for lunch.

"Papa, they said I can take you outside for lunch, if you would like. The place where I got you the cake has a big buffet. Your coat is here, and there is a shawl to put over your legs."

Yes, let's escape! Did I say that out loud enough, he wondered? It doesn't matter. Every fiber of his being shouts "Amen!" Out the door, down the street, onto the subway, into the city. But we should stop at the restaurant first. A little fish and a lot of chocolate cake, and you keep asking your questions. It would give him time to wander and wonder, anticipating the next room she might open. I'll take my Bible. He's not surprised when she hands him his Bible. Now she grabs the wheelchair and pushes with gusto. That's the way, he thought. Most people treat me like porcelain. He likes the daytime nurse, an African, she pulls and pushes him like he's a man. Off they go.

He feels imperious. Is that the right word? Imperious? Imperial? Impervious? With an almost jaunty smile he greets everyone along the way, like a general inspecting his troops. He feels the wind in his hair, he isn't even outdoors yet.

She chatters along the way, not too concerned about the various impediments they bump into. In his armored throne the bumps are adventurous. It seems everyone watches, greets, some even envious as they waltz their way to the corner restaurant. The crowds part like the Red Sea, a prime table awaits. The feeding of the five thousand begins for him, as it did long ago, with a little fish. The chocolate will come, he knows this. In the Bible story, he remembers, there was more than enough for everybody, twelve baskets of leftovers. From his seat he carefully observes the dessert section. Yes, there is plenty of chocolate cake left over, waiting.

"This would make a nice heaven, don't you think?" He's positively beaming.

It's her turn to wander inside, and to wonder. Take a deep breath, she knows, smile, don't look concerned, find that train of thought. Let's see: food, fish, escape, heaven.

There's a link there somewhere, this does feel like a test. But I like it. Keep smiling, bide my time, hope he beats me to it.

He does. He has entered his study in his memory palace, the walls lined with books, the only marriage that lasted long enough.

I got it! she almost bursts out loud. Bible stories, of course, that's the link. Bible stories.

"Papa, do you have a favorite Bible story? I know, you probably have 50, or 500, or whatever, but you must have some favorites."

"My father used to preach from the Book of Daniel. Shadrach, Meschach, and Abednego. You know that story? He nicknamed them Shake-the-bed, Make-the-bed, and Into-Bed-You-Go, so we would remember them. They refused to deny God, so the King threw them into a fiery furnace. But God saved them."

That was worth two bites he decided, and took them.

"And Daniel in the lion's den, the same story. People wanted to be faithful to God, the politicians wanted the people faithful to them. God stood with the people. I liked those stories."

He took a deep breath; perhaps he was tired. Were the memories wearing him out, the words outside, the thoughts inside? She sensed both and wondered if she should stop.

"Are you tired, Papa? Should we go back?" He looked like he was thinking deeply. She'd been warned that at such times he could appear angry but that he wasn't, it was just his pensive face, her mother said. A pensive face. The actor in her liked that, so she let it linger.

She looks happy, he thought. I shouldn't ruin that with my stories. I grew up with a hard God, very stern, demanding, like Dickens, lots of Great Expectations. That thought broke the pensive face, he began to smile again.

"I used to preach," he told her, straightening up in the chair. As he ate the last bit of chocolate he thought about how to use the right words correctly, how not to diminish her smile. "When I was younger I preached about judgment. Like my father. But then I realized justice mattered more to me than judgement."

She didn't dare move a muscle, nothing to interrupt this surprising flow.

"Your grandfather, he pointed a finger at the individual. Me, I wanted to point a finger at society."

My grandfather! So he does know me, almost, close enough. Now she has the pensive face. This is pretty heavy stuff.

He started to hum an old hymn, she listened carefully as if she should know it. "That's a nice song, Papa," not wanting to give herself away. He lifted his hands as if conducting, and sang,

Tell me the stories of Jesus
I love to hear
Things I would ask him to tell me
If he were here.

A lady at the next table turned toward them and joined in:

Scenes by the wayside
Tales of the sea
Stories of Jesus
Tell them to me.

She and the lady nodded empathetically toward each other. "Your grandfather is a man of God," the lady said, "and you are an angel." They looked at each other and said at exactly the same time, "are you Indian?"

"East Indian," the lady laughed, "by way of London. Now Flatbush. I must say that around here, so many are West Indies, the Caribbean and cricket, and all such."

The lady touched him on his arm, "You are a blessing," as she stood up to leave. "One day we should go dancing."

"Yes, if my granddaughter lets me," he said with a hearty laugh.

Somehow she has gained a generation. It was worth the trade.

If it can be said that a man in a wheelchair had a bounce in his step it would be true as she wheeled him out of the restaurant and up the hill to the nursing home. To those walking by, the old man and the young woman seemed to be gliding, a tandem fueled by smiles. Up the street, into the building, past the guards, into the elevator, onto the third floor, down the hallway, past the nurses' station, into his room, settling him with three newspapers and a cup of tea, ready for the day ahead.

She laughed to herself. This all seems like a Chagall painting, with floating Rabbis and Christian symbols, old Europe in New York, an earthbound mysticism. This was more than she expected, and just what she wanted.

"I have to go, Papa. I have to get back to college."

"Really? Oh, of course you must. You, in college, right in this city. Isn't that something." There was obvious pride in his voice.

"I was expelled from college. Someone saw me go into a movie theatre in Scollay Square." He reached behind, opening the drawer on the bedside table, taking out his wallet. He gave her $10.

"No, Papa. I don't need money. But thank you very much."

He refused to be refused. With conviction he pressed it into her hand, as they kissed goodbye. "Go to a movie," he whispered, conspiratorially. She was too happy to cry.